HOLIDAYS & HEARTSTRINGS

WINTER WONDERLAND SERIES

ALEXANDRA BANKS

WILLOW HOUSE
Publishing

Book design by Alexandra Banks

Cover design by Covers by Canea

First Edition: December 2025

ISBN – eBook – 978-1-7643423-0-8

ISBN – Paperback – 978-1-7643423-1-5

Also by Alexandra Banks

Rosewood Ranch Series
Tough Love
Heart & Hope
Saving Grace
True North

Fire Island Series
Tender Heart
Fire Heart

Love in the City Series
Sassy Love
Burning Love
Tangled Love

YOU
ARE
HERE

Winter Wonderland Series
Holidays & Heartstrings

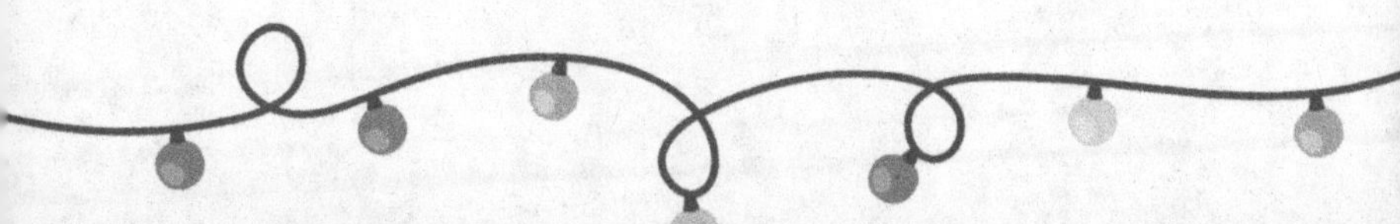

For every weary heart at Christmas time . . .
Merry Christmas baby.

Holidays & Heartstrings

playlist

I'LL BE HOME FOR CHRISTMAS
TATE MCRAE

PICK OUT A CHRISTMAS TREE
DAN + SHAY

OLD MEMORIES ON CHRISTMAS
ALICIA KEYS

MERRY CHRISTMAS DARLING
CHRISTINA PERRI

LIKE IT'S CHRISTMAS
JONAS BROTHERS

ROCKIN' AROUND THE CHRISTMAS TREE
KELLY CLARKSON

SLEIGH RIDE
GWEN STEFANI

AULD LANG SYNE
PISTOL ANNIES

ONE MORE SLEEP
LEONA LEWIS

YOU MAKE IT FEEL LIKE CHRISTMAS
GWEN STEFANI

AUTHOR'S NOTE

TW –

This book contains difficult scenes and recounts. For the full list of trigger warnings please visit - https://www.alexan dra-banks.com/ebook

The location, topographies and personas of the places and characters in this story have been fictionalized. They may not accurately represent actual location and terrain.

You can access the playlist here!
https://open.spotify.com/playlist/
3txgxbLwHOeL6fIVhofukW?si=
vDyyZAP9SR6yGFThkTt-eQ

Holidays & Heartstrings

CHAPTER
ONE
CELESTE

The long-haul bus doors hiss and snap shut behind me, snagging my favorite scarf in its maw. *Shit!* The oversized wheels turn.

The bus rumbles away from the curb. I teeter on the icy sidewalk before spinning my way out of strangulation and avoid being dragged alongside the bus by my winter wardrobe.

Finding my balance eventually, I watch as my scarf flies alongside the bus, in all its freedom and glory.

I press my frozen fingers to my neck, now burning from the quick departure of what was my favorite colorful scarf.

Well, welcome home to you, too, Grafton.

A beat later, the small-town Main Street closes in with all its quiet charm. My two overnight bags, stuffed with every single possession that wasn't nailed down or of ques-

1

tionable ownership in the tiny studio bedroom that, up until yesterday, I lived in with my roommate of seven years, drop to the sidewalk.

A defeated sigh slips out as I take in the tiny town that hasn't changed one bit in the last ten years. I breathe in the cold air as it nips my skin and brightens my nose to a rosy pink hue and sends my ears burning.

Grafton, Vermont—home to the childhood I was only too happy to leave behind for the bright lights of Chicago. Now, it's home to a population of seven hundred and two.

Still tiny.

Still freezing in winter.

Still stunningly beautiful with all its heritage buildings and New England charm. And . . .

Still like watching paint dry.

Now bursting with Christmas color despite it barely being December 1st.

The folks I grew up with mull about, like the day I left a decade ago is still in progress. They go about the same things, in the same places, and in the same ways.

Can't blame a girl for wanting to escape a real-life *Groundhog Day* situation, can you?

But as vibrant and fun as life was in Chicago, it was also stressful and expensive. And mostly, much too far away from the only person left on this planet I care about—my father.

Which brings me to the reason I'm back.

My chest aches at the thought. And I hope, even though the hope is a completely useless waste of time, that he's having one of his increasingly rare good days, and he'll remember me.

I pray for that, eyes drifting shut as the quiet hustle of the small town that raised me hums softly. I pluck up the bags and decide to hike the four blocks to the small dirt road that leads to the bigger houses on the outskirts of town. Crisp snow crunches under my boots. As I make my way through Main Street, currently adorned with every holiday trimming in dark green and red known to mankind, and then the sleepy streets, my breath curls ahead of me, as if leading the way home.

The blue skies show no signs of the blizzard that apparently took Grafton by surprise, judging by the mile-high snowdrifts and yet-to-be-shoveled driveways. Amber-tinted leaves cover every newly turned tree, the few evergreens dotted among the streets between the deciduous stand over front yards like dutiful soldiers in pairs flanking every white-picketed gate. Grand heritage homes that take more upkeep than the White House, no doubt, stand proud in the center of each family's small allotment of land.

"Yoo-hoo! CC, darling, is that you?"

That didn't take long.

A gray-haired woman in her sixties presses a hand into her lower back as she straightens, garden shears in hand, delight scrawled all over her face. Mrs. Matheson, my fifth-grade teacher, who by the looks of it, has been immortalized. Most likely the frigid weather preventing her from aging, or the fact that she's the biggest square a small town has ever had the privilege of housing.

"Hey, Mrs. Matheson, how's the garden?"

"Oh." She waves a hand at me, shaking her head. "Frost killed most of it. Same every year."

"That's a shame," I call back, not slowing or changing course.

"You home for the holidays? Your father will be so pleased, bless his heart."

"Yup." I point an awkward finger, still gripping my bag, toward the direction of said home and offer up a small smile. "See you 'round."

I catch a glimpse of her front door featuring an oversized golden wreath, complete with angels and bells.

Urgh. Christmas. An annual reminder of all the things our family has had to live without for so, so long . . .

"Of course, honey! Say hello to your father for me."

Absolutely not.

Even on a great day, making mention of anyone who's not close family or in his everyday life only serves to send him into a confused stupor. Mrs. Matheson can keep her kind gestures, along with the rest of this town. I may have been living through his everyday via long-distance, but Marie, his live-in caretaker who has been with our family for over a decade, calls me twice a day, morning and night.

And since I'm the youngest of three, at the sprightly age of thirty, and the only one without a 'serious career' according to my brother, well, here I am.

Leaving Main Street, I trudge my way through the side alley that leads to MacKelvie Lane, home to one of the original families of Grafton and our only neighbors in this tiny town for as long as I can remember.

Old Mrs. MacKelvie's apple pies are something to behold. I'm sure she bakes in edible gold to glam up her pies . . . They're that stupidly good.

Mrs. MacKelvie has always been old. I swear she's been seventy for thirty years now. However, her grandchildren—who rarely visit—would be around my age now, from a quick running calculation. Her children all left for the city, one after the other, leaving her alone after all those years.

This time of year, I can almost smell the apple, cinnamon, pie crust, and . . . Smoke?

Shit.

I pick up the pace. My bags slam into my thighs as I close in on the two grand homes side by side. I'm out of breath. And a whole lot confused. Outside the MacKelvies' is a large drum, burning, legs of antique chairs sticking out of the top.

Hey, what?

Okay, that's not—

The front screen door of our house snaps.

Marie's face lights up as she crosses our wide porch,

drawing my attention to my own home. Leaning on a colonial-style column, she folds her arms over her chest, her smile widening. Not a Christmas decoration in sight.

We love Marie.

Without my mother, our father lost interest in the world around him. We were so little when she died. At least, I was little when Marie started taking care of us like her own children not long after we lost our mom. Then she went from caring for us to caring for my father in one seamless transition.

I drop the bags the second I make the porch, and she pushes from the column and envelops me in one of her warm hugs.

And for a minute, she feels like the mother I grew up without.

"Welcome home, Celestia."

Her nickname for me. A combination of my name and the stars of the incredible night sky that floats above Grafton in the wintertime.

"It's so good to be home." The words almost get stuck.

She holds me at arm's length. "He's waiting for you in the sunroom. It's a good day. Even better, now that you're here."

I huff a breath of relief, trying to stem the emotion that comes with the fact my father should recognize me.

I reach for my bags, and she shoos me inside before popping back out. To grab my luggage, I assume.

I walk into the foyer that has always felt far too formal

for our family. The house is huge, even for a family of five, then four. Until Marie came stepped in, at least. She was Mom's best friend.

"Hello?" I call out as I travel the corridor, a library flanking my left and the sitting room on the right. I know I'll find my father in the sunroom at the back of the house. His favorite place.

And my mother's before it was his. Every story he tells me about her, she was sitting in the sun's rays or the moon's beams, painting or sculpting. The great Leticia Black. Her work still hangs around town; at least it did last time I was home. I guess I took after my mother with the artist gene. But the fact that I haven't sold a single painting worth enough to keep my bills paid and my career afloat tells me the genetics I received are somewhat watered down.

I find Dad in the chair by the southern windows.

Rounding the chair, I touch his shoulder before sitting on the ottoman in front of him. "Hey, Daddy."

His face lights up with delight. A beat passes and his brows frown. "Tisha, you're supposed to be at the studio. Did something happen?"

I've been assumed to be worse people than my own mother, and in his defense, I am her spitting image. Dark hair, brown eyes, wide smile, small nose, and petite frame. Not-so-petite personality.

"It's me, CC, Daddy."

His face curls with confusion, then morphs to embarrassment. "I'm sorry, honey—"

"No, don't be. I've been honing my Leticia Black style for a while now."

He chuckles, but the frown doesn't ease. "You do look so much like your mother, sweetheart. Sorry, I got confused."

"I'll take the mistaken identity as a compliment. Anyway, how have you been? Marie looks great, she's keeping you on your toes, hey?"

"Your mother is always busy organizing my days." He leans forward, hands gripping my knees. "All this old man wants to do is read and nap. She won't hear of it." The smile that widens his face is spectacular. And I put my mother's inability to resist my father down to that one feature alone.

"I bet she does, Daddy."

He's mixing up the two most significant women in our family. But he's not wrong. Marie was pretty much my mother figure. She took care of us. In return, she had a home and a family that would always do anything for her. But nobody could ever confuse the two . . .

"Can you do this old man a favor?" he asks.

"Anything." I squeeze his hands, now back on his lap.

"I'm parched. Bring my tea, will you?"

I stand and dot a kiss to his forehead. "Of course, be back in a sec."

He smiles before picking up his book.

Mark Twain.

Again.

I guess there are perks of not remembering things, after

all. What I wouldn't give to read my favorite books for the first time over.

I wander through the house and into the long galley kitchen. The black-and-white tiled floor has seen better days, as have the countertops and cupboards. Marie stands at the counter, preparing the tray loaded with a tea pot, two cups, and the sugar pot with two teaspoons.

"How did it go?" she asks.

"Okay. He mistook me for my mother for a second there. Not a big deal."

"Lots of people do, until they remember . . ." The cheeky expression that sprung over her face fades with the last few words, and she gives me an empathetic expression, plucking up the tray.

"What's going on next door?"

"Ah, that would be your new neighbor."

"What? What happened to Mrs. MacKelvie?" My face is widened, hands gripping the counter. Surely, she just moved into the nursing home or something. Marie would have told me.

"I was trying to find the best time to tell you, without your father overhearing and—"

"Tell me what?"

"She died."

"When?"

"About two months ago."

"Two months! Marie, why didn't you tell me?"

"I don't know . . . I'm always with your father, I didn't

want him overhearing and getting upset. They were friends."

"Well, he's going to figure it out eventually."

"True, I guess he might."

"Then who is burning the drum?"

She pulls a face that looks suspiciously like a cringe. But I'm sure Marie hasn't used that kind of expression ever in her life. "Her grandson."

"Oh" is all I can say.

"Yes, oh." She rolls her eyes and mine nearly fall out of their sockets. "He's disposing of all of her *outdated* furniture. Apparently."

"You've talked to him?" I lean over the counter, mouth agape.

"Briefly. Your father was outside, without any clothes on." She picks up a teacup not on the tray and sips it.

"Oh." I can only imagine the encounter.

The secondhand embarrassment it brings shouldn't be so intense. I know it's not his fault. I know it's just his condition . . . Still.

I know nothing about this person next door. Everything about our neighbor is new. And I have the overwhelming urge to protect my father from him. Regardless.

"I popped your bags in your room upstairs. Let me deliver this, then we'll catch up." She walks from the kitchen with the tray. I amble through the house to the central staircase. The mahogany railings still smell the same, woodsy and ancient like the house itself. Ascending the stairs, I take in the photos of our family. Mom and the three of us. And ones of just us kids.

Some of them have Marie in them. Some don't. Which doesn't feel right.

When I make it onto the first-floor landing, all of the doors are open, the windows closed against the cold. My room is the last door on the left.

The soft, worn carpet runner that leads the way dulls my footsteps as it always has. Sound echoes off the cream walls with brown polished wooden trim around doors, skirting boards, and windows. When I cross the threshold to my old room, I sigh. Padding across the equally worn floor rug over hardwood floors to the bay window and seat, I push back the curtain.

Next door, out in the backyard, is the new neighbor. Another burning drum and a few odd pieces of furniture are on the lawn, now sentenced to a timely death by fire also.

Despicable. If old Mrs. MacKelvie could see the fate of her precious pieces now . . .

Shaking my head, I turn away, unable to watch the ultimate demise of the old chairs and whatnot that she loved and cared for dearly. The generations before ours valued their possessions, realizing their hard-won value. A sentiment that is apparently lost on whoever has taken over next door.

Smoke curls outside my window.

Barbarian.

I cross to the bed and flop onto my back, letting my gaze

stagnate on the ceiling. The space is a time capsule hell-bent on preserving my childhood the best way it knows how. Without change or interference.

But one thing is for sure.

This still feels like home.

CHAPTER

TWO

QUINTON

"Eat your greens or no ice cream, little lady."

My daughter, love of my damn life and spitting image of the woman who couldn't be bothered to stick around for her, pouts. Her dark chestnut curls bounce as she shakes her head, dark eyes narrowing over her pretty nose and tilted-up chin.

"Yucky."

Her five-year-old face bunches with disgust.

I fold my arms over my chest, leaning back on the ancient dining chair. It creaks with my weight. Maisey's eyes widen at the noise. The sooner I get rid of all this decrepit old junk, the better.

Every damn piece of furniture in this house is an accident waiting to happen. And since nobody on either of the town's buy-sell-trade sites wanted the junk, I'm stuck with it. Until I can burn it all, bit by bit. The town dump

13

wouldn't take it on principal, something along the lines of the fact that it would be like trashing the great Agnes Elizabeth MacKelvie.

Small towns . . . Good Lord.

Besides, I didn't know her, really. My mother left our father when we were young, only going back here once a year for an annual visit. Never long enough to be meaningful. Just long enough to check it off the 'not-a-bad-ex-daughter-in-law' list.

But the chance to raise my little girl in a place like this, where she can be safe and happy, trumps every feeling I have about map-dot towns. This one included, with its family history and apparently massive shoes to fill, thanks to Agnes.

So, we're burning it all. And as soon as I have it cleared out, new furniture should just about be here, if the estimate from the local furniture store is accurate. Besides, the ash will be good for the gardens I plan on installing when the warmer weather comes in spring.

"No ice cream, remember," I warn, and she harrumphs but plucks the floppy green vegetable between two tiny fingers and holds it up for inspection.

She winces as she brings it closer to her mouth. Taking a small bite, she pretends to gag.

I know it's pretend because she used that same tactic last week with the lettuce on her burger when we made home-made chicken burgers, as per her request. Guess she wasn't anticipating the crunchy layer of watery goodness.

"Hmmm. Dis so gross, Dada." Her mouth is full of mushy greens.

I shake my head. "Not with your mouth full, Maise."

She swallows, wincing again dramatically. "There, done."

Her eyes sparkle as she places her cutlery in the center of her plate, like the little lady I'm trying to raise her as.

"Good job, kiddo. Just let me finish up."

"I can get yours, too, Dada."

She slips off the old chair and runs for the kitchen before I can object.

I finish up my meal and take our plates to the sink. Scraping them off, I glance up.

A light on next door catches me by surprise. Hank's room is on the other side of the house . . . As is Marie's.

Nice old guy. Shame about his condition.

I dunk the plates into the soapy water, washing them down as Maisey plonks the ice cream tub on the counter, climbing onto one of the stools. She pulls out the drawer, finding a scoop before her little tongue pokes out in concentration as she sends it through the middle of the ice cream. Her curls hang around her shoulders as she leans in further, so determined.

The ice cream is hard, and the scoop flings out of her grip, hitting the floor.

"Oh shit," she hisses.

"Maisey Emmaline MacKelvie. Manners."

She snickers softly, climbing off the stool to pick up the scoop before handing it to me to wash off under the tap.

I hand it back to her, and she mounts the stool with determination anew.

"Save some for your old man, hey?" I chuckle, pulling two bowls out of the cupboard and setting one by the tub just in time as she rolls the perfect ball over the edge and into it. It lands with a plop, and she giggles, cracking the smile that blooms over my face so damn wide.

My heart squeezes in my stupid chest.

It's moments like these I'm glad her mother decided to leave and go alone.

I don't think I could have handled it if she had taken Maise with her to Vegas. The other side of the fucking country. Still, the fear that one day she'll change her mind and come to collect always lingers in the back of my mind. My gut churns, as if on cue, every time that particular thought springs back to life. Luckily, it doesn't come up too often.

"More?" Maisey asks.

I snap my gaze to the overflowing bowls.

"Think that'll be good." I take the bowls to the sofa and flick the television on as she puts the ice cream away and runs for the living room. She's in my lap a second later. "Daddy, you forgot the spoons again." She giggles, turning on my lap. Her little hands wrap around my jaw as she whispers, "What would you do without me?" Her forehead presses to mine.

"No idea," I say softly. And I damn well mean it.

God knows how I will make it through a day when she starts school next week. After two weeks of settling in, it's time she started at her new school. My little contracting sidekick, she has more knowledge and skill than half the guys I work with. More sass, too. Someone's got to keep us in line. The guys on-site adore her. The pink hard hat was a hit when she first started coming to work with me a year ago, when I could no longer afford babysitters or day care.

One of the downfalls of owning your own business. The highs are great, the lows can ruin you.

Maise's gone and back with two spoons a beat later, curled up against my chest again. I flick it over to her favorite show about rescue dogs and try to eat my ice cream one-handed. She's clean and sweet, all bathed and in her pajamas. And when the bowl slips in her lap twenty minutes later, I slide it to the side table and pry the spoon from her grip.

"Bedtime, my girl."

I carry her upstairs, tucking her into the enormous canopy bed in the room she chose for herself. Knows her mind, my little girl. Of course she does.

I glance out the window to the drum. The load has been reduced to coals that now glow and flicker with the occasional lick of flame. Under the night sky out here in middle-of-nowhere Vermont, the sight is something to behold. I just hope I can make this work. That business picks up, and we get settled here for good.

Maise needs a good, stable home. Somewhere to grow and play. In the center of chaotic Boston wasn't it. Grafton being a far cry from the city is one of its most attractive features.

I adjust the blankets around her shoulders and kiss her hair before turning out the light and closing the door almost all the way shut. I pad across the hall to my own room. The master.

This is the most impressive house I've ever lived in, and the room is incredible. More space than my old apartment. And this room is also home to an ornate king canopy bed. Matching nightstands. Luckily for this old bed, I'm too tired to disassemble it and haul it down the stairs to meet a fiery end.

I shower and pad downstairs to lock up and turn out the lights. The lights next door are burning still.

I frown, hesitating for a moment. But I know Marie is there, and she would call if she needed help.

Weary, I stretch, heading up stairs. By the time my head hits the pillow, my eyes are drifting shut.

"**D**addy, I'll be fine. Go to work, okay?" Her hand presses against my stubble. I'm squatting at the front doors to Grafton Elementary School. A crabbity old teacher, Miss Francis, stands behind Maise, waiting with a not-so-patient face.

"You sure? We can ditch this joint and play hooky . . ."

Her little brows drop quickly. "No, uh-uh. You can go play hooky, but I'm going inside to make friends."

I chuckle and rise to my feet. "Good for you, kiddo."

"Did you get the forms from the admin office, Mr. MacKelvie?" the old bat asks again.

"Yep." I wave the forms that are still clutched in one hand at her as her mouth pinches and she ushers Maisey inside.

"Have a great day, my girl," I utter, watching the large double doors swallow my flesh and blood who's currently dragging my goddamn heart on a threadbare string behind her. The Christmas wreaths that hang on each door jostle as they thud shut, and I'm left outside in the cold.

Scrubbing a hand down my face, I loose a breath and trudge through the light, fresh snow to my truck. Once inside, I crank her over and toss the forms onto the bench seat. The sooner I get to site, the sooner I can get back to pick Maisey up.

I turn onto Pleasant Street and head back to Main. It takes all of four minutes to get to the Grafton Inn, where we are currently doing renovations in the dining area. A medium-size job, nothing major. But keeping the old heritage style the building has keeps us on our toes.

When the truck rolls up outside the inn, I take a second to appreciate the grandeur of the architecture, the stoic white columns, the wide porch, the multipaned windows, and the whitewashed stone exterior. It's a stunning building, and one of the landmarks of this small town.

Currently, it's decorated with wreaths, boughs of holly, and bright-red blooms hung under the eaves of the first-floor balcony that spans the entire front. The porch itself is littered with ornaments and stylish decorations that make the space look like a winter wonderland. Which it kind of is, this time of year. The snow flanking the building and covering the grounds really sets it off.

Incredible.

I kill the engine and haul my ass inside, knowing the guys will be waiting for me. I can hear the steady thrum of power tools before I make it to the dining room. Helen, stationed at the reception desk, gives me a big smile and a wave. "Morning, Quinton, how did she go?"

Her blue eyes follow me as I wander past, heading for the dining room. "Better than her old man." I give her a lopsided grin.

Helen sags against the desk with a sigh.

Is she okay? I hesitate for a second until crimson blooms over her cheeks and she excuses herself, turning away to busy herself with the computer at her desk.

Okay . . .

I see the guys hard at it the second I clear the double doors to the dining area. The space has been closed since we started, and as Miranda, the co-owner, likes to remind us all every afternoon, every day we take to revamp the old space, she is losing money.

I'm well aware of the difficulties of small business—currently running my own.

"Morning, boss man, almost done sanding. We'll clean this up in an hour or so and get onto the finishes."

"Great. Time is money, boys."

They all roll their eyes at me.

Ronan, the eldest on our crew in his early forties, simply shakes his head. Caleb, our part-time guy who owns a legit reindeer farm, chuckles into his respirator mask and sends the sander back along the banister he's working on. And then there's Sebastian, the quiet, moody one of the group. He fires up the industrial vacuum and makes short work of the fine dust before rolling up our drop cloths behind him. Man of few words and one of the hardest workers I've ever had.

I make a start helping Seb, rolling out the cloths as he goes. Everyone does every job on my crew, no hierarchy and no special favors. If it has to be done, it gets done. Period.

We're an hour into the work when my butt vibrates.

It takes a second to realize what on earth is going on. When Ronan tilts his head at me, eyes fixated on my ass, I realize what he's trying to say over the noise.

My phone's ringing.

Plucking it from my back pocket, I swipe the semi-familiar number and step outside, careful not to drop fine sanding dust over the inn's foyer floor. "Hello?"

"Mr. MacKelvie?"

"Yup, speaking."

"You will need to come and collect your daughter. There's been an incident."

Ah, fuck.

CHAPTER

THREE

CELESTE

I stare in disbelief at the face I've known for most of my life. My mouth is gaping, that much I know, as I try my best to process the words that just left Marie's lips.

"I'm leaving."

"No, absolutely not." My face is twisted, and I'm suddenly parched.

I cannot do this on my own.

She tilts her head with an empathetic smile. "You will be fine. Besides, I need this, CC. I need a break, maybe some time to find something in life just for me?"

God, I'm a horrendous human being. This woman has loved and cared for a family who is not her own for decades, to the detriment of her own wellbeing in some phases of our family life. Now, she wants to find a little piece of solace for herself and all I can do is think about how this affects me.

Lord.

This is why I'm single.

This is why my life is so dysfunctional. The heart of an artist, the maturity of a child.

How on earth am I supposed to be my father's sole caretaker and fix up this falling-down house? Not to mention earn some semblance of a living to keep us afloat.

"Marie, please. Please stay a little longer, I don't think I can do this on my own. It's been ages, and he's much worse than last time I came home."

She folds me into a hug. "If I don't leave now, I never will."

She's right.

There's never a good time to break the ties to the ones you love. Never.

"I guess," I say, following with a long sigh.

"Anyway, you and this old house have unfinished business, missy."

Um, okay . . . now I'm confused.

But she continues, "Well, actually, I should say you and your mom's old studio have unfinished business."

"Ah, that. I'm no Leticia Black, I'm afraid. My art is never going to support me. The universe has decided it's better as just a hobby."

She tilts her chin down with an incredulous look. "Not with that attitude, you're not. You think your mother gave up when things were hard? She fought for her art, and the whole town got behind her. Think about the opportunity you have here. You now have time, space, and people to back you. Coming home was a good move for you, hon."

I sit, stunned, lost in my head now reeling with possibilities, responsibilities, and this grand old house. All of which are now mine to do with what I can. It's a heady feeling that comes with a weight I'm not used to bearing.

But one glance into the corridor at the beaming smile on my mother's face as she holds one of her artworks in her grip, her overalls splattered with paint, has me willing to take the chance on myself. One last time.

Maybe I can do this?

A new start, with a fresh plan.

Hell, what do I have to lose?

Absolutely nothing.

Marie reappears midway into my deep musing, startling me with a vigorous handclap. "Right, so now that's settled, I want to give you the rundown on a few things to help you start off on the right foot."

She pulls a bulging folder from the top of the fridge and slaps it onto the counter.

One word adorns the spine. *Hank.*

She has a file on my father?

"This is all Dad's stuff?" I ask. She spins it around to me and pushes it closer.

"Yes, mostly. Routines for each day of the week, to accommodate his hobbies and appointments. The meals I make that have been set by the naturopath and dietitian. His medication schedule. And the collection of recipes for the foods on the menu and a few he just loves that I didn't have the heart to deprive him of, despite what the doctors say."

I flip the front cover open and find a neatly set out contents page. This woman has this nailed.

"And you do all this, every single day?" I ask, utterly impressed but, at the same time, terrified.

"I don't cook every single meal every day, just the assigned ones to make sure he gets all the nutrition to support his health."

Good Lord, I'm screwed.

First, I'm the world's worst cook, and second . . . I'm overwhelmed caring for myself, let alone all of . . . this.

"Marie, I can't do this. I mean, I really can't."

I'm practically begging her to stay at this point. If she leaves, the fate of my father is basically left to chance. Me and routines are not well suited. I couldn't even hold down a part-time gig, let alone something so time-consuming and never-ending.

With a sigh, she sits beside me on a counter stool. "Honey, I know this is out of your comfort zone. But that's kind of the point."

"What do you mean?"

"Your brother and sister . . . they think this is what you need. Direction, structure, and focus. Meaning something apart from your own life for a change."

Those sniveling, dirty snitches.

I cannot believe they went behind my back to Marie about this. I know I was struggling, but aren't all artists?

It is literally the status quo.

"You have so much potential, CC. But we all feel the structure will help you. And I really do need a break."

I slump on the stool like she plucked the wind from my sails. And deep down, I know she is right. My siblings—who will die slow and painful deaths for this utter betrayal—I hate to admit, are not entirely wrong.

I was floundering. Nothing kept my attention. Whether it was work, guys, or whatever latest project I was trying to pump out.

Nothing.

"Think of it this way. You now have a real chance to take a break from the chaos and focus on you and your father. Find your inner peace before you find out what you really want to do with your life." Marie dots a kiss to my forehead, like she used to when I was little, and rises from the stool.

"I'm going to head out early today and get some errands of my own done. Look through the binder. The schedule is laminated and clipped to the front cover. Start with that so you know what's up for his next meal and round of meds, okay?"

"Sure," I say, but the word is soft. Almost lost.

Marie disappears as I thumb through the pages, leaving me to process the world's most subtle family intervention. And like most other interventions, I don't get a choice. Because if I don't comply, my father will be left alone. Or with some stranger who doesn't understand or even care.

That thought alone steels my determination.

I huff a sarcastic laugh. That didn't take long. And I know I've been played. They knew I could never say no. I've always been daddy's little girl.

Setting back my shoulders, I turn to page one and start learning every nuanced detail about my father's life.

"Shit! Shit. Shit. Shit!"

The handle of the pot of boiling water slips through my hands and hits the floor. I manage to mount a stool before the steaming liquid reaches my bare feet. Fucking hell.

Only when I hear a faint holler from the sunroom do I clamber off the stool and edge my away around the steaming liquid studded with the potatoes I was supposed to be cooking. They now currently look like slimy, muted mounds splattered around the black-and-white tiled floor.

"Dammit, why can't we order in like civilized people . . ."

I pad down the hallway as the hollering continues.

"Coming, Daddy," I holler back, hoping he's right where I left him before I set out on the world's most difficult cooking accomplishment—mashed potatoes.

He's not.

Hovering by the window and peeling off his underwear, he points to something outside as I pick up the pace, grabbing a throw rug from the sofa en route. "What are you doing, Daddy?"

He spins back, now stark naked, his face lit up with excitement. His finger presses to his lips. "Shhh. Tish and I are going skinny-dipping in the lake out back. Don't wake up her folks, girlie."

Ah, he's twenty-three again.

If only.

"It's too cold outside to go skinny-dipping. And the lake is on the other side of town, remember?"

"No—no, I just saw her outside." His brows drop, confusion washing over his face the way goosebumps have his skin. "You . . . why did you call me Daddy?"

Ah, fuck.

I was given the rundown before Marie left this afternoon. I was explicitly instructed to remain neutral when he's having a bad moment. Nothing to suggest time or place. Stick to generic responses and redirect to something he can do like read, watch the game, or go for a walk.

Fuck.

The thoroughly confused look on his face is like a vice grip around my heart. Why on earth did my family think this was a good idea? I'm not good at this. Not in the slightest.

"Sorry, Hank. Let's pop your clothes back on, okay?"

"Yes, yes," he murmurs, wandering around the room, taking it in as if for the first time.

I pick up the underwear and hand it to him. He simply stares at it in his hand.

It's not the first time I've had to help my father with something this personal, but it still makes me feel a little uncomfortable. And then a whole lot guilty. The man wiped my butt and changed my diapers. Mopped up my vomit and dried my tears. The least I can do is care for him now, when he needs me.

So I squat and hold out the underwear. He steps into it in an automated motion, one leg after the other. The pants go next and then I slide his shirt back on, buttoning it up. When his vest and coat are snug around his shoulders, I give him a smile. "There you are, all warm."

He tilts his head. "Thank you, love."

But I can tell by the way his eyes are mostly vacant that he doesn't recognize me today.

That's okay, I know who we are enough for the both of us.

"How about some soup for lunch?" I ask, knowing Marie's everlasting stock of her famous pea-and-ham soup will be sitting in single-serve portions in the freezer.

He brightens. "The little breadsticks, too?"

He remembers *that*.

I chuckle and say, "Sure. Breadsticks, too."

He nods, sitting in his reading chair. He plucks up Mark Twain. "I've been meaning to read this one for months, you know. Hope it's as good as everyone says." He opens to the first page and leans back in the chair, swiping his reading glasses from the side table as he settles in.

Me too, Daddy, me too.

I pad back to the kitchen and tug the freezer open. Sure enough, single serves of the world's greatest comfort soup sit stacked in the top of the frosty space. I pull two out and reheat them in separate bowls before hunting for a box of breadsticks.

My head is inside the deep pantry cupboard as the doorbell rings.

"Who on earth . . ."

I head for the front door. I can hear my father's voice before I even open it.

"Get your hands off me, lad!"

Shit.

I swing the door open to find my naked father, wrapped in a throw blanket that I'm pretty sure isn't ours, being held by a tall guy around my age with light brown hair. His deep blues are drawn with concern, his grip unwavering on my dad's arm as he tugs the cap from his head. "Sorry, Hank was wandering through my backyard. Thought you'd want him back. Quinton. I live next door."

My father rips his arm from Quinton's hold and stalks inside. His gait is a little wobbly as he shivers under the blanket.

"Um, thank you."

"Yeah. I'll tell you what I told the last caretaker. Lock your doors and hide the key."

My mouth gapes.

What an ass.

Luckily, the man who raised me has already drifted down the hall when I say, "Fuck you."

I slam the door in Quinton's face.

And to think Marie thought he was nice. Urgh, what a heartless, self-centered—

Something crashes inside the house as an explosion booms from the kitchen. I take off running toward the sounds, only to find the blanket discarded further down the hall.

Good Lord, what now?

FOUR

QUINTON

"You want to tell me what happened?" I hug Maise into my side as we sit on the back steps of the house two hours after my neighborly encounter. We watch the drum of furniture pieces burn down as the last of the day's light sinks over the horizon. Luckily for my daughter, I was able to usher Hank back to his house without any drama before she came outside.

The new caretaker was—

"Nope."

"Maise . . ."

"She started it," she mutters.

"She started what?"

"Being a bully to Casey."

"And Casey is . . . ?"

"The girl I was buddied up with for my first week."

"Ah, okay. And you finished it, I gather."

Her hands snap to her hips as she looks up at me, serious as hell. "Sure as shit did."

"Maisey Emmaline MacKelvie," I growl at her for the language, but I can't seem to wipe the proud damn grin from my face. So to hide it, I turn away, pretending to study the neighbors' houses.

"Sorry, Daddy. She just was so mean. She made Casey cry. And I only started there, and—"

She's getting herself all worked up over this.

"Hey, kiddo. You were defending her. But if we are going to stay at that school, you can't hit people."

"Why not? What if they deserve it so bad?"

I huff a laugh and shake my head. "No, kiddo, not even then."

She pouts like I knew she would.

And I return my gaze to the windows of Hank's house. I hope he's okay. I was taken back by the woman who opened the door. She is definitely not Marie. Much younger. And those damn eyes, those curves.

Fuck.

I hope she's good to Hank. He was dealt a shitty hand with that disease.

". . . Daddy?"

"Hey, sorry, what's up?"

"Who was the old man in my snuggle blanket?"

Shit, I just grabbed the first one I saw. I didn't even realize it was hers.

"Hank from next door, he gets confused sometimes.

Thought it was summer and was wanting a swim. I'll get your blankie back tomorrow."

"Why is he confused?"

"His mind can't stay focused, and he forgets."

How else do you explain dementia to a five-year-old? 'Cause I have no idea.

"Oh, okay."

She pops off the step and wanders around the yard, collecting leaves and twigs for who knows what. I pull out my phone and check business emails and the accounts, to make sure outstanding invoices have been paid. Nothing worse than having to tell the guys payday will be late because a customer bailed or paid late.

The accounts are looking a little sad, and after a little digging I find three invoices that are outstanding. *Typical.*

I send reminder emails and pluck up the beer I brought out here after dealing with Hank. It's still cold, thanks to the current Vermont weather. Just another thing me and Maise will have to get used to.

"Hello?" a feminine voice calls from the front of the house. It's barely audible from the back steps, and I wait a beat. Maybe it was next door?

"Anyone home?"

Nope, that is definitely my coming from my porch.

I push up and walk through the house, opening the front door.

Dark eyes look up at me. Her fine features are framed by dark wavy hair. Her pert little nose has already started to redden and her pretty pink lips are currently pursed. A hand juts toward me, Maisey's blanket folded and resting in her palm.

"I washed it, just in case you're wondering."

"I wasn't."

I don't know what it is about this woman, but my usual fully functional language skill set is nowhere to be found. Apparently, it ran off with my manners. I stare at her, unable to pull my gaze from her face.

She shifts on her feet with a huffy laugh.

"Right, so much for friendly small towns. I see that was just a nineties thing." She turns on her heel and stalks from my porch, crunching her way through the snow back to Hank's house.

Her front door slams.

Creature of habit, I see.

I close my door and walk back through the house, tossing the blanket onto the sofa as I go past. Maise comes flying into the house a second later, claiming to have found a pet bird that looks like it's half frozen. Great, now we've got to try and resuscitate the damn thing.

Fuck my luck.

She lays the bedraggled thing on the kitchen counter and races off to find something. The bird is in shock, by the looks of it. Probably won't last the night. A heartbeat later, she reappears, distraught.

"I can't find a shoebox!" She spins around, hands flying upward. "Daddy, we *need* a shoebox to keep her warm!"

Sighing, I tug my coat from the hooks by the door. "Stay here, I'll be right back."

Maise is fussing over the bird as I step outside and pull the door shut behind me. The first flakes of the evening's snowfall start to drift downward as I crunch my way toward Hank's house. He's the closest neighbor for half a mile. If he doesn't have a shoebox, we ain't getting one.

By the time I make the front porch, curiosity has the better of me, and I'm half hoping the new caretaker will answer the door.

Not that I'm interested.

I knock, brisk—all business.

The bird. Right, the bird.

Not that I have any desire to get into to anything serious with a woman after the last disast—

The door swings open.

Instantly, the pretty face that greets me twists with annoyance.

"Come to check if I locked the doors and windows, lest you're inconvenienced again?"

I would laugh at her sassy first words, but heat floods my neck and face. I didn't mean to come off as inconsiderate or uncaring, but apparently that's exactly what I've done.

Nothing new, I suppose. I've been told time and time again I'm too blunt.

"Ah, no." I rub a hand behind my neck, letting my gaze wander behind the beautiful brunette in front of me, almost searching for Hank. I'd much rather talk with him, if he's having a good night. It changes so fast for him, almost hourly, so—

"Did you come over here just to snoop? Or *just* to stare?"

Huh.

Right.

If I'm blunt, she's sarcasm and intolerance personified.

"You know what, forget it." I turn on my heel and make for the steps.

The door slams behind me.

I shake my head and huff a disbelieving sound. Well, that didn't take long for her to hate me. Talk about getting off on the wrong damn foot.

It should bother me that my new neighbor doesn't like me, that her bitterness has been constant since we met. But for some reason, by the time I get back to the house, I can't wipe the smile off my stupid damn face.

Maise is sobbing into her pillow.

Birdy, as she so eloquently named it, didn't make it. She was gone by the time I got back from Hank's. Honestly, I doubt she—at least, we think it was a she—would have made it through the night. Birds are always touch and go, and in winter . . . the odds are bleak.

"Maise, you did everything you could. And we were with her when she closed her eyes. She was warm and loved at the end. More than most creatures ever get, kiddo. You did good."

She wails into the damn pillow and my heart tumbles from my chest.

Fuck.

Sitting on the edge of her bed, I rub a hand over her small back. She's had a long, dramatic day. And every inch of me hurts seeing her upset. And not all of those tears may be for the bird. She was so excited to start a new school, and I imagine today did not go the way she hoped it would.

My beautiful girl. My sweet baby . . . God, I just want to fix every problem, save her from every hurt.

But I know I can't. I'll never be able to do that.

Best I can do is give her the skills to take care of herself.

Lying beside her, I drag the mess of curls away from her face, and she opens her eyes. "I really thought today would be so great, Daddy."

Her little chin wobbles.

"I know, kiddo. I know." I hug her into my chest and her small, fine fingers wrap around the opening of my shirt.

With a sniffle, she lifts her gaze to mine. I lie on the pillow as she presses her palms to my chest. She feels cool against my skin, always chasing my warmth. Coming to my bed in the middle of the night when she was younger.

I'd wake up with her curls plastered over my face, her little body pressed up against my side, drool over my pillow. But there are worse ways to wake up.

I offer her a reassuring smile. "Today is done, but tomorrow is all ours."

She rolls her eyes at me, and I chuckle.

"I guess," she whispers. Her hand brushes over my days' worth of stubble. "So scratchy, Daddy."

"Must be time for a beard, then."

Her face twists with disgust. "No way!"

I chuckle and pull her close, smothering her while I rub my knuckles in her hair. "Tickle time, then, hey?"

She squeals, batting her little hands into my chest. I release her a little way and poke her ribs playfully as she wriggles on the bed, kicking her legs around.

Much better.

It takes her a while to register that I'm no longer tickling her, and she settles, her laughter fading as I pull her duvet over her. I brush her hair from her face and plant a kiss to her forehead. "Night, my beautiful girl."

She snuggles in, tugging the blanket up higher. "Night, Daddy."

"Love you, Maise."

"Love you, too."

I rise from the bed and pad across the room. When I turn out the light, I lean on the doorframe, watching her cuddle her bear and close her eyes. Double-checking the thermostat is warm enough, I push from the door and walk into the hallway.

"Dada?"

Backtracking, I pop my head in her doorway.

That gets a small giggle. "Can we do the tree tomorrow when I get home from school?"

"Sure, kiddo. I'll pick you up, and we can head to Caleb's and pick a tree."

Her eyes are lit up. So much for being sleepy. "A really, really big one?"

"Absolutely."

"Night, Dada."

"Goodnight, Maise."

I pad back down the hall to my room, exhausted from running a small business, raising an energetic, curious kiddo, and making a new home for us in a new town. It all takes a very real toll by the end of the day. But when I lie my weary body, those dark eyes from the woman next door won't budge from my mind.

Her sharp words and annoyed expression only serve to make her more endearing in a way. But she has made it very clear—she does not like me. At all. And with the vitriol that spilled from her tonight, the feeling is mutual. The last thing I need right now is a shitty neighbor, so I'll keep my distance.

It's a pity our house and theirs are the only two on this nondescript street in the outskirts of Grafton. It would have been nice to have a friendly face around. Folks to be neighborly with. Grill, have a beer with at the end of a long day, or lend a cup of sugar to. All that small-town stuff that was part of the attraction of moving here.

Kids for Maise to play with would have been great, also.

I close my eyes, rubbing my hands down my face as I second-guess every decision I've ever made. My latest big change is front and center of the self-doubt that rises with each thought, more depressing than the last.

How can we ever know if we're doing the right thing by our kids?

Who knows how the school situation will pan out . . . One thing I can try to give her is good neighbors. I can try again, maybe apologize for a rough start and beg for a do-over?

One can only try, right?

"Do we have to get a tree this year?"

My father's face drops into a frown from the passenger seat of his old truck. I shift the stick into drive and pull out onto the street. It wasn't long ago that he would be sitting here, taking me to the Christmas tree farm. Funnily enough, also a reindeer farm . . .

If the kids ever realized that the reindeer are not, in fact, waiting for Santa's call—like Caleb has insisted on telling kids this time of year ever since he took over the family farm —they'd be horrified to learn their beloved deer are food.

"Yes, I know you kids have had a thing about Christmas after your mother, but a tree is nonnegotiable." He looks out the window. He's having a good day. So far . . .

Then, "How will Santa leave you gifts without a tree? That scooter you want isn't going to fit in a stocking."

And I'm seven again, at least in his mind.

I remember that Christmas. It was the first after Mom died. And I did not get the scooter.

"You alright, pumpkin?" he asks.

That name is about as old as the letter I sent to Santa about the scooter . . . And I can tell today is going to be a constant back-and-forth between then and now for him. For us.

I remind myself he's healthy—physically—and still here with me. And I focus on that, the good parts. The fact that I still have my dad.

Emotion clogs my throat as we turn onto Main Street. I grip the wheel harder, and the burn on my hand from making us scrambled eggs and bacon this morning smarts, like my skin just met the hot skillet all over again.

I hiss and flick the turn signal to turn onto a side street before heading out of town to the farm.

"Is Marie meeting us there?" Dad asks.

"No, remember, she's having the day off." I offer a small smile.

"Oh, I must have forgotten."

Yes, Daddy, it happens a lot.

A few minutes later, we slow and turn onto a gravel road that leads to the Christmas tree and reindeer farm, Maple Acres. The truck rattles over the cattle guard, and we jostle in our seats as I slow down, looking for a spot to park among the many vehicles already here.

Two barns sit on either side of the driveway, one lit up

with people walking through, dragging their trees behind them. The other barn is flanked by a tall white fence. Behind it, the deer watch on as folks appear from the barn and make for their trucks and larger SUVs to cart their trees home.

Strings of fairy lights light up the outside of the tree barn and snow still litters the ground, giving the whole place that winter wonderland look. I park and kill the engine. Double-checking our coats are buttoned up, I slide my arm through my father's.

"Shall we get the biggest tree we can find this year, pumpkin?" he says, leaning closer, his words excited but soft.

"Sure."

When we make it inside, the barn is much the same as I remember it from last time, which was years ago. The large, open space is mostly hay storage with a small booth where you pay for your tree. But some upgrades have taken place. A stall selling cider and hot chocolate sits to the left of the entrance. And the ceiling is lit up with more strings of fairy lights, setting the old barn in an ambient glow. The hay-littered floor of the barn crunches underfoot as we make our way through the groups of people chatting, dragging trees, and enjoying steaming beverages.

The place is just so . . . happy.

"Here for a tree?" a young girl says, holding out a tag on a string. "This is to claim your tree. Caleb will cut it down and help you load it, if he's not too busy." She doesn't stick around for an answer, turning to greet the next group of people through the door.

I slide the card and string into my pocket as we move further inside the barn.

"Hank!" A man calls from across the barn. He closes in on us fast, and I scramble to remember his name. Mr. Henderson who runs the hardware store? I'm pretty sure. It's been almost ten years, but I remember stealing mouse traps from his shelves once on a dare.

Hopefully, he doesn't remember.

"Howard, nice to see you," Dad says.

And I smile, not just because it's polite, but because my dad is having a rare lucid moment. I treasure every one we get, knowing how fleeting they are.

"Great to see you out and about. We've missed you of late."

Confusion washes over my father's face, but he corrects it, mostly. "How's the wife? Still baking those Christmas cookies this time of year?"

Mr. Henderson's face falls as fast as my father's moment of clarity fades.

Mrs. Henderson died the year before I left home.

"I'm sorry," I say to the man who is standing stunned, his mouth moving but producing no sound. "We should get a tree before all the good ones are gone."

I offer him an empathetic smile.

He simply nods. "Of course. Shout if you need a hand loading it into your truck."

"Thank you." I slide my arm through my father's, and we walk through the barn and out into the field of Christmas trees. Rows and rows of snow-dusted pines stand like dutiful soldiers. It's incredible.

Some tower over us, others barely reach my shoulders.

How on earth will we ever choose?

A few folks stop to say hello, mostly welcoming me back home for the holidays. My father wanders through the trees as I try to get away from a girl who was in my grade in elementary school. I feel bad that I can't remember her name. I watch as he stops by a medium-sized pine. It's got excellent foliage coverage and an almost perfect shape where it stands.

"Excuse me." I force a smile to the woman saying hello, not really bothering to see if she returns it, as I stride through the symmetrical forest and to my father's side. "Find a good one?"

"This one's a beauty, Tish. This is it."

I take in his lit-up face before casting my gaze to the tree. It surely is.

"Well, this one it is!"

He beams at me. I slip the card from my pocket and bend down to tie it around the tree's base. Murmuring comes from the tree. Okay . . .

Either I've lost my mind, or—

A hand slips around the trunk of the tree, rope wrapping around the bark.

What?

No, no way. This is our tree.

I spring up and round the tree. A large half a man is sticking out the bottom of the tree.

No, out from under the tree . . .

"Excuse me, this is our tree." I snap my hands to my hips.

A small child appears from nowhere, coming to stand beside the man crouching under the base of the pine. She's bundled up, wearing a beanie and an oversized coat. A scarf covers most of her face, leaving her dark brown eyes that are now narrowing as she stares at me.

Shaking her head, she says, "Nope, we saw it first."

"Ah, we have been standing here for, well, at least five minutes, this is our tree."

The man shuffles backward, standing before brushing off his knees and then clapping his hands together. Blue eyes pierce right through me as his gaze alternates between the kid and me.

"Our tag is on. So, I guess it's ours now."

"No, no. We were standing right there." I round the tree pointing to the snow-covered ground marred with our footprints, like a crazy person.

Brows lower over his blues. "Look, there's like hundreds of other trees to pick from, just—"

"Hold up!" I raise a hand, stepping closer. A huffy laugh of disbelief sends a cloud of breath from my lips. "You're the guy from next door."

He folds his arms over his chest, raising a lone eyebrow. "And?"

He obviously recognized me before I did him. *Shit*.

The little girl's eyes are wide and pleading as she shakes her head at me for the second time in as many minutes. "Please, can we keep the tree? We've been here for ages. You have no idea how fussy my daddy is."

I narrow my gaze and lean down a little. "Did he make you look at every single one before you were allowed to pick?"

She rolls her eyes with a groan. "Yes."

I snap up straight. "Seriously, every single one?"

"She's exaggerating." He tilts his head, giving the girl the side-eye, but his lips tilt up like he's trying so damn hard to tamp down a smile.

"Fine, you keep the tree. This time."

"Thank god for that," the girl says, slapping a hand to her forehead dramatically.

I chuckle. I like her, she's got a great sense of humor. She'd need one, having this guy for a dad.

I take a second glance at the man in front of me. He's actually not that ba—

"See, that wasn't so hard, was it? Helping out a neighbor." He gives me a smirk that lights up his stupid face.

You have got to be kidding me.

Urgh . . . Nope. I was right the first time.

What an ass.

"Hey, where did your daddy go?" the girl says, turning on the spot.

Oh shit.

I spin around, glancing through the rows where people wander, all bundled up and unidentifiable unless you're looking right at them. I take off through the rows. "Hank?"

Dammit.

Pressure builds in my chest. I was supposed to be taking care of him. Keeping him close. The notes in the binder on outings has everything outlined. Stay close. Keep a visual on him at all times.

But no, I was too busy arguing over a stupid stinking tree . . .

Tears burn behind my eyes. It's that torturous feeling you get when you're little and you lose your parent, your hand slipping from theirs in a crowd of bodies, followed by your stomach sinking, your panic rising to fill the void it left.

But this time, the panic is laced with guilt.

Trees fly past as I hurry through each row, one after the other, calling for my father like a little girl. The strangled sound of his name feels too raw. And I know I'm freaking out, but despite every person I pass and every section of the farm I cover, the overwhelming feeling only grows. I have no way to rein it in.

Passing the last row, I slide to a halt when I reach the white wooden railing. The end of the tree field.

"Shit! God, how could I be so selfish?" I spin on the spot.

"Well, it is the time of the year to think of others. Maybe you temporarily forgot? Easy enough to do." The low voice startles me, and I turn toward it.

I find a bundled-up man, beanie over his dark hair, blue eyes lit up. Is that an axe in his hand?

It's now I read the name stitched over the Maple Acres logo on his vest.

Caleb. I almost didn't recognize him.

"You looking for something in particular?" He tilts his head, studying my face.

I huff out a sigh, but it wobbles. "My father."

His brows drop. "Did you try the barn?"

"Oh, no. I just kind of freaked out and started running around like an idiot." I slide the beanie from my head and wring it through my hands.

"You were worried about him?"

"You could say that," I utter, an icy cloud puffing from my lips.

"We talking about Hank Black?"

"Ah, yeah."

"Celeste?"

He steps forward.

"Yes?"

"Huh. You probably don't remember me, I was a few grades above you in high school."

"Oh, yeah, sure."

It all floods back. The face, the name. The fact that he's taken over his family farm. Makes sense. Not all of us were as self-absorbed as I was to run off to the city and never look back.

"Let me just grab this tree out and I'll give you a hand to look."

"Oh, you don't have to."

"Nah, it's no trouble. Besides, he's always done a lot for our family. And this town."

And the guilt is back as I realize my father spent his life helping others and being a great friend. And I missed it.

But the sentiment sounds about right. He's always been a kind and generous man.

I swallow past the emotion that Caleb's words evoked. Once he's shouldered the medium-sized tree trunk, we walk back through the rows until the barn is in sight.

"How is it being back?" Caleb asks when we get closer to the barn. He glances at me, but his gaze swings to where my father sits on a hay bale, a small bundled-up child next to him as they both sip the mugs in their hands.

"It's a big change. But I'm happy to be here."

It's almost the truth.

"Well, I see he's safe and sound." He tilts his head Dad's way. "You need a hand with a tree too?" he asks as the folks waiting on their tree take if off his hands.

"Ah, no. We're still finding one."

He dusts his hands on his jeans before leaving with a nod and a bright smile. I close in on my father and find him sitting with the little girl from the tree scuffle before. "Here you are."

"Hello, darling. Have you met my friend?" Dad says, taking another sip.

I plaster a smile on my face and offer her a small wave like we've just met. "Hey."

"Daddy will be back soon with our tree. Did you find one?" the little girl says.

Yeah, the one you stole.

"Not yet," I say with a forced smile.

Footsteps close in behind me, and I glance back to see the thief himself carrying our tree over his shoulder. Because of course he is. I resist the temptation to roll my eyes and scoff at him.

"Ready, kiddo?" he says, frowning as he takes in the three of us together.

"Yep." His daughter jumps up. "Can we decorate it straight away when we get home?"

"Are the decorations stolen, also?" I whisper to myself.

He turns toward me, tree balancing on his shoulder. "Guess you'll never know." He winks at me before taking his daughter's hand and giving me his back.

Now I roll my eyes at him, letting the scoff free.

They walk through the barn, paying for their tree before disappearing through the front.

"Come on, let's find a tree." Dad hugs an arm around my shoulders. "I have a feeling about this Christmas, darling."

Sorry if I don't bank on that feeling of yours, Daddy.

CHAPTER
SIX
QUINTON

The tree is up, the not-stolen decorations adorning its fresh boughs. The last element was just wrapped around—the string lights that Maise has loved since she was a baby. I hold the remote out to her, and she flicks the switch.

Nothing happens.

"Oh no!" Maise whines.

"Batteries must be dead. Hang on, I'll grab some more." I pass her the remote as I walk into the kitchen, ready to rummage through the drawers. Papers, matches, bottle tops, and enough miscellaneous junk to start a small fire. No batteries.

Hell. This is Maisey's favorite part of decorating the tree.

"Maise, we need to go and grab some more batteries. Get your coat," I call as I open the fridge and take stock

55

quick. May as well get the few things on the grocery list while we're out.

Maise appears with my coat in her hands, hers already wrapped around her and done up, her beanie pulled down over her curly hair, and snow boots over her jeans.

"Come on, Daddy, we need to get these lights sorted."

All business, my little lady.

I chuckle at her and pull on my coat. We slip out the front door and I pull it shut. Crunching our way over the snow, we load into the pickup truck, and I fire her up. Two minutes later, we're pulling into the Village Store. Maise is out of the truck before I can kill the engine.

I follow her in as she strides around the small shop, hunting for batteries.

She has them in her hand by the time I find my few items—bread, milk, and eggs.

"Found them, Daddy. You good?" she says, gaze landing on the items in my hands as we round the end of the aisle.

"Someone's in a hurry to get those ligh—"

I slam into something soft and fragrant.

Maise gasps.

Something hits the floor, a wet sound following . . .

I look down to find a fluster of wavy dark hair awash over—

She's squatting, cursing under her breath.

Celeste.

Just our luck.

It didn't take long for the small-town grapevine to be

overwhelmed by talk of the prodigal daughter who returned home to her ailing father. And with a few strategic vague questions to my crew, mainly Caleb, I got all I need to know about Celeste Black.

Maise lowers to her knees, trying to help contain the mess of juice and . . . Is that a to-go coffee?

I shelve my items and squat. "Ah, sorry about that."

Her brown eyes flick up, narrowing when she recognizes me.

"Maybe you should watch where you're going?" she retorts.

"I was."

She huffs a breath. "Apparently not."

The store staff appears with paper towels and a mop and bucket a heartbeat later, and the three of us step back, letting them clear up the mess. But now my items are stranded on the shelf where I left them.

We'll have to wait.

"You live next door to us," Maise says with a beaming smile.

Celeste drops her gaze to my daughter's happy face. "That's right."

"Did you want to come over? We're lighting the tree."

"On fire?" she says with a smirk.

Maisey cocks a hip. "No, with lights."

I've never been prouder. My girl has sass that could take down a marine.

Celeste fights a smile. Maybe there's a reasonable woman in there somewhere . . .

"Yeah, no, Maise. We should get back."

Celeste glances at her empty coffee cup. "I'm just going to . . ."

She wanders off.

And shit, now I feel bad.

Should I?

A small hand tugs at my coat. "Daddy, buy her another coffee. It's the right thing to do at Christmas time."

"Is it now?" I raise a brow.

Hers lower as she adds a firm, "Yes."

Damn me for raising this little lady right. I rub a hand behind my neck, assessing the situation from my vantage point. That is to say, hoping I can stall long enough for Celeste to leave.

No such luck. She grabs up a shopping basket and heads for the fridge section. Most likely replacing the juice she just lost.

"Daddy," Maise warns.

"Fine, but your lights are going to have to wait."

"I can wait. It is Christmas time, after all." She folds her arms, her final gesture ushering me to my doom.

Internalizing a groan, I cross the small shop to where Celeste stands, picking out some of the better winter fruits before placing them in her basket.

"So, ah. Sorry about that, back there I mean. Did you— would you . . ."

What the fuck?

I clear my throat. "Let me replace your coffee?"

It sounds more like a question than an offer.

Celeste doesn't bother meeting my gaze as she continues picking up apples and turning them over in her hand. "No thanks."

"Come on, let me replace it."

"I'm good." She still doesn't look at me.

"I realize we didn't get off to the best start, but—"

She turns, pinning me with her dark gaze. "You think?"

I don't respond, and Celeste moves on to the vegetable section. Great, she's going to make it hard.

Fucking Christ.

It's embarrassing how this woman I barely know gets under my skin so damn easily.

I glance back to see Maise tapping one foot.

Why did I take the proper route and raise a strong, independent girl? It's currently biting me in the ass. Big time.

"Celeste."

Not turning back, she sighs, her shoulders rising and falling. "What, Quinton."

It sounds like a statement, not a question. And my name on her lips takes me by surprise.

"How do you take your coffee, at . . ." I glance at my watch. "Nine at night?"

"I take it alone. Without an annoying man who thinks it's acceptable to steal an old man's Christmas tree, without a man who thinks it's perfectly acceptable to burn his grandmother's prized possessions at the holidays in front of the town who loved her. It's—"

I raise a hand, and she stops, snapping her mouth shut.

"I get it."

"Do you?" She steps forward, basket at her side, stopping with only inches between us as deep browns burn up into my gaze.

Holy fuck, she's . . .

I swallow as my body livens at her proximity. The first time that's happened in, well—

I glance at Maise.

That long.

"Done staring? Or is that just another one of your miserable traits?" Celeste whispers.

I let my eyes shutter closed as I take a step back, glad to be out of her space. I think?

"So, no coffee," I finally say after opening my eyes.

"Nope."

I retreat, shoulders sagging as I return to a frowning Maisey. "Sorry, kiddo, I tried."

Her little face twists under disappointment.

I make my way to the shelf I abandoned my items on. Swiping them up, we pay and head out. Almost to the door, Maise stops to pull up her socks that have slipped down in her boots. I make a mental note to buy her new ones as I wait.

We make the door, only to be met with a flurry of brunette waves as I come shoulder to shoulder with Celeste.

She rolls her eyes at me before schooling her face into a smile for Maisey.

So the grinch does have a heart.

A little taken aback, I make space and let her through.

Maisey follows her through the door but heads for our truck. I open the door for Maise, and she climbs on up. I set the bag of groceries in the footwell before closing her door.

Rounding the front of the truck, I spot Celeste in Hank's old pickup they took to Maple Acres. She's on her phone, the screen illuminating her face, the angles accentuated in the blue-white light. She's all elegant cheekbones and pretty, pouty lips. Her hair tumbles over her shoulder as she tugs her bottom lip in between her teeth in what I imagine is concentration.

"Daddy, the lights?"

"Oh, sorry. We're going."

Maisey's gaze strays to where mine was planted a second earlier.

She smiles as she presses her palm to the window. Outside, snow starts to flurry around the small convenience store. Our cue to get home.

I start up the truck and shift her into reverse.

Maisey's stare bores into the side of my face.

"Okay, what?" I say, eyes on the road.

"She's pretty, Daddy."

"Who?"

"Really?" Her arms fold across her chest.

"Celeste?" I say, feigning ignorance.

"Yes, Celeste is pretty."

"Not as pretty as my favorite little lady." I wink at her.

She rolls her eyes. "You're getting old."

"What? No, I'm not."

"Obviously you are if your eyesight has gone already."

Jesus.

I chuckle, not even getting a chance to stifle it. My girl is perceptive as hell. And Celeste is . . .

Well, Maise is right about one thing—our new neighbor may be a complete pain in my ass, but she's stunning. I'll give her that.

Since it's Christmas.

Yeah, that's it, a Christmas nicety.

By the time we get home, the snow is falling in steady waves. I help Maise out of the truck and head upstairs with our few items. After shucking our boots, Maise makes a beeline for the tree while I put the eggs and milk in the fridge, leaving the bread on the counter.

Food stored away, I wander to the living room to find an almost bursting Maisey, remote in hand. The room is dim, ready for the big moment.

"Ready?" she squeals.

"Ready, kiddo."

"Countdown! Ten, nine, eight, seven, six, five, four . . ."

I take over. "Three, two . . . one . . ."

"Merry Christmas!" we holler at the same time she flicks the switch, and the room comes alive, the tree blazing in every hue of the rainbow. The star on top emits a warm golden glow, dousing the ceiling.

I wrap my arms around my daughter, and she climbs me like a tree as she twists in my hold. "Isn't she so beautiful!"

"She is. You did so good."

She snuggles into my arms, her head dropping to my shoulder as she yawns.

"Bedtime, clever girl," I whisper.

"No . . ."

"Maise, you have school in the morning."

"Fine. But remember I went to bed without a fuss even after staying up so late." The second the words leave her mouth, she looks sheepish.

Shit, it's late.

I'd been so caught up in the tree and the incident at the store, I lost track of time.

I narrow my eyes at her playfully. "Noted."

"You mean it? Can I stay up later on the weekends now?"

"I'll think about it."

"Yes!" She claps her hands together and I carry her up the stairs. She may be fiercely independent most times, but at the end of the day when she's tired or when she's scared or hurt, she's Daddy's little girl.

And knowing how fleeting the years we get to spend with our children are, I'm not one to look a gift horse in the mouth. I plan on making every moment count while she still needs me.

I make the last step, and her head lolls.

She's asleep already. I lay her on her bed, removing her coat and jeans and tucking her into the warm covers. I dot a kiss to her forehead and pad downstairs to lock up and turn out the lights.

At the front door, I flick the locks. Just before I turn back, lights swing into Hank's driveway. His truck pulls up, the engine idling for a moment before it splutters out.

Celeste steps down from the truck, her groceries in hand. Snow litters her dark hair in a stark contrast. She slams the truck door and trudges through the snow and up onto the front porch. The outdoor light comes on automatically. I'm glad it's still working. It was one of the first things Marie asked me to help out with after we moved here.

As if sensing me lurking and staring like the damn creep I'm being, Celeste turns and glances at my house. I swear our eyes meet, and I back away from the door. Hank's front door slams. I chuckle, but there's no humor left in it, just an overwhelming realization that I'm at a crossroads that I have no idea how to navigate.

And the sight of Celeste burns into my frozen mind as I pad up the stairs toward the end of another long, exhausting day as a single parent, business owner, and world's shittiest neighbor.

I should try to fix that.

It's Christmas time, after all.

My gut flips at the thought of being near Celeste again.

But I can only imagine the fire I'll come under from

Maise if I don't try to give this new neighbor thing my best effort.

She's all heart, my girl, even more so at Christmas.

Her current excuse for every damn thing she wants me to participate in.

Fucking Christmas.

CHAPTER
SEVEN

CELESTE

With my father currently occupied at his biweekly physical therapy session that goes for two hours, I sit in the town library hoping to find something to read, information on caring for a family member with Alzheimer's, and maybe something on home maintenance. Despite Marie giving me the rundown and the Godzilla of all binders, I still feel out of my depth.

Christmas is not helping.

All the expectations of participating in town events and seeing people I haven't spoken to in over a decade are resurrecting my long-lost anxiety, that's for sure. As if the universe is indeed laughing at me, my old principal from elementary school wanders past, stopping short when she notices me at the long central table in the center of the library.

Yeah, right in the center of the library was probably a bad idea.

"Celeste! How lovely to see you home."

"Hey, Ms. Kincaid."

"It's Mrs. Semple now," she says with a wink, flashing me her ring finger.

"Oh, I didn't realize. Sorry."

She pulls out a chair, dropping the three books that were in her arms to the table.

Just great.

"How have you been? It's been so long. How's your dad?"

I don't know which one to answer first, so I go with the easiest. "Dad is doing okay, I guess."

She tilts her head the way people do when they feel bad for you. "You're a gem to come home and take care of him. I know that must be really hard. To leave a career behind and move back to the tiny town you—" She squeezes my hand.

I ran from. Was that what she was going to say?

"So far, it's been nice to be home, but I'm not sure I'm cut out for the caretaker gig. I'm kind of terrible at it, actual-ly." The last few words fade out.

"You know what you need? A project of your own to think about. It can feel very isolating when work or what-ever is the only thing you've got going on. Take it from me."

The way her face strangles back something that looks like grief tells me all I need to know.

"How long?" I ask softly.

"Five years now. And Steven was a godsend. And now I don't know what would have become of me without him." She glances at her gold-and-diamond adorned finger.

"I'm sorry," I utter, trying to not let emotion get the better of me. One of the downfalls of being a creative—I feel everything so intensely, even if it's not my own.

She scrunches up her nose and forces a smile, her hand clasping over mine. "The school is looking for someone to help with the art program. They have taken on a rather ambitious project for Christmas Eve. Your help would be much appreciated."

"I don't know, it's hard to leave Dad alone."

"I understand, but think about it, will you? For you, more than anything else, okay?"

I nod.

She rises from the chair and waves goodbye as she hugs the books to her chest before disappearing into the history section.

How am I supposed to focus on anything else but the full-time, twenty-four-seven job of taking care of my father? I'm barely managing as it is.

I flip open the book I found on his condition, checking that it covers what I need to learn. When I find two that seem to have a comprehensive overview on Alzheimer's, I set them aside. Next, I flip through the pages of a home maintenance manual. Diagrams and detailed instructions on how to do just about anything to upkeep and fix your home resides on the pages. I set that one on the take-home pile, too.

After applying for a new library card—who knew they expired?—I bundle up and brave the new fall of snow and take a walk down Main Street. Each shop or building I pass resurrects memories I'd long forgotten. But unlike the memories filled with friends and my siblings, of that feeling of freedom that someone on the brink of discovering the big wide world has, now I feel the heavy regret of not having accomplished the things I'd set out to do.

My art.

All the travel I wanted to do, the places I wanted to visit. The cultures I never immersed myself in . . .

The art and people.

Now anchored to this small town by my heart and soul in the shape of the man who raised me, any hope I had left is fleeting. And that burns, so much so that I stop in the snow, staring into the window of the Gift Shoppe on Main Street.

Only, I'm not staring at treasures for my loved ones . . . Just at my reflection that feels as stagnant as my future.

I never thought this was how my life would turn out. My art was everything.

But maybe I was just a big fish in a small pond.

Guess now I'll never know.

With a sorrowful sigh, I turn and head back to the truck parked by the library. Unlocking the driver's side door, I toss my bag onto the passenger's seat and climb up. My head hits the steering wheel. The horn blares. I jerk back, my heart racing.

Shit.

Maybe Mrs. Kin—Semple was right. I need a hobby. A distraction. Something to think about other than all the ways I've failed myself and am currently failing my dad.

Putting the truck into gear, I drive home, a tiny sliver of hope sparking to life as I turn onto my street.

The binder lays on the counter, open to the Thursday meal plan, the corresponding recipes for the day tabbed in a color-coded pink. Parental care for dummies.

That's me.

The dummy who is having trouble deciphering how to make beef meatloaf and steamed dark greens.

I reread the recipe for the third time. Do I put the eggs in on top of the meat, or in a separate bowl? Lord, who knows.

The counter is now littered with ingredients, measuring cups, spoons, a bunch of herbs—some of which I've never heard of—and the basics like flour, pepper, salt, and garlic powder.

A loaf pan. I need a loaf pan . . .

What on earth is a loaf pan?

Urgh, Marie, how could you do this to me?

"Need a hand?" a small voice chirps from the doorway.

I jump, dropping the wooden spoon that was in my hand.

"Oh my god, where did you come from?" I ask the young girl in the kitchen entrance.

"I heard you swearing from next door." She's trying and failing to flatten a cheeky smile.

Oh shit.

I mean, dammit.

You shouldn't swear around kids, I'm guessing.

"Sorry, I'll keep it down."

"That's okay." She walks in, slipping onto a stool like she's done this before. "I can help."

"Um . . . okay?"

"I'm Maisey. What are you making?"

"I'm Celeste."

I turn the binder around to face her, and she slides it closer, nodding. "Yum!"

"Really?" I wring my hands through the apron covering my jeans and sweater.

"We'll make it yummy."

I chuckle and she smiles up at me. I like this kid. She's got spunk.

"You read the recipe, and I'll do the grunt work," she says, sending the binder sliding over the counter toward me.

"You can't read?"

"I'm in kindergarten, lady, so that's a no."

I can't help laughing at her, but I try to tamp it down, pressing my lips together and holding a hand over my mouth.

"Got it," I finally manage to say.

"So, what's the first instruction in the recipe?" she asks.

I raise a brow. "You sure you can't read?"

"Yep. My dad reads, I cook."

"Ah, of course."

I read the first dot point out to her slowly. She grabs the ground beef and dumps it into the bowl with the herbs, salt, and pepper just as I instructed.

We work as a team until the bowl is full of what looks like a mushed-up brain with green flecks and the random diced vegetable poking from the mass. It looks . . .

"Your oven, it's not on." Maisey looks at me, surprised.

"Was it supposed to be on?"

"You always turn on your oven before you start cooking."

"Oh shoot, really?"

"Yeah, it's okay, this will wait. Baking is a whole different story, though," she says with an exaggerated eye roll.

How is this little girl better at life than I am?

"Okay, how do I turn it on?"

"You serious?" Maisey's brows fling toward her hairline.

"Yeah, my mom—I never learned to cook."

"Oh, okay." She looks as if she's figured something out. "Turn this knob to bake. This one does the temperature."

Marie was great at taking care of us. We never went without, but she didn't teach us the things a mother would, I guess.

I've never cooked. Which was sometimes an issue for roommates I had, and not for others. Takeout is always welcome, and I was happy to buy it in lieu of cooking. A choice that is now coming back to bite me.

When the oven dings, I open the door and slide the loaf pan into the middle shelf under Maisey's supervision. She holds a hand out for a high five when I shut the door. I slap my palm to her small one and she wanders toward the pantry cupboard, her head disappearing a second later. "Got anything to eat?"

"You mean apart from meatloaf and dark greens?"

"Yeah. Yuck, spinach is so gross."

I pull open the drawers until I come across a bag of chocolate chip cookies. "How about these?" I ask.

She pulls her head from the depths of the pantry. On seeing the cookies, she plants herself onto the stool by mine. I bust open the bag, and we dig in.

Milk, we need milk . . .

"Milk, hon?" I ask.

She scrunches up her nose at the endearment but answers, "Sure."

I grab two glasses and the milk from the fridge. After pouring our milk, we dig in again.

My name is a faint call as I scarf down the cookies, chatting away with my new friend and cooking buddy.

Dad.

"Sorry, I better see if he's okay." I rise from the stool, finishing off my milk.

"That's okay, I'll wait."

"Be back in a bit."

I stride to the living room, where I find my father worrying over the tree we bought the other day. The three lines of tinsel wrapped around the girth of it glitter in the afternoon sunset.

"You okay?" I ask, coming to his side as he rubs a hand over his sweater, his head shaking.

"No, this tree is . . ."

"It's lovely."

He gives me a deadpan look.

"Come on; it's fine. We barely even do Christmas, anyway."

His mouth opens in something like shock.

"Daddy . . ."

Confusion floods his face.

Shit.

I will never get used to this. I scramble to think of something to fix this. "My daddy is, ah, coming with more decorations next week. It'll be beautiful then."

"What day is he coming? I need everything to be perfect for Tish this year, after all that happened last year."

Last year?

I rack my brain, trying to think of something bad that happened to my mother besides her dying when I was seven.

But we were so young, and Dad didn't talk to us about her much after she died. We figured it was because it was just too painful.

Now?

"Is she okay now?" I ask, hoping his memories are clear enough to be understood. Desperate to know more about my mother.

"She will be, lass. Marie will make sure of it."

Marie?

He turns his attention back to the tree, his jaw feathering. "This Christmas has to be a good one. It just has to be."

Oh, Daddy.

The front screen door whines and then slaps closed. Oh shoot, I forgot about Maisey. Leaving Dad to the tree, I walk toward the sound of heavy footsteps now thundering down my hallway.

Not Maisey, then.

CHAPTER

EIGHT

QUINTON

The sunset illuminates Celeste's hair, setting her against the world's most beautiful time of day, only to pale in comparison.

Nope, not here to gawk at the new neighbor.

"Maisey here?" I snap out.

Hell, if I'm friendly right now, I'm not only the creep that was watching her the other night, but I may as well say goodbye to my gonads. Because despite my attempts at keeping this woman out of my damn head, she's lodged in there.

Her face twists in annoyance.

Good.

"Kitchen." She waves a hand, sarcasm dripping from the gesture.

After helping Marie a few times, I know where it is. I

77

walk down the hall and take the second left. I find my girl perched on a stool, dipping a cookie into a glass of milk.

"Oh hey, Daddy," she says, beaming like she didn't just give me the fright of a lifetime by disappearing from the house without a word.

"Something wrong with the cookies at home, Maise?" I fold my arms over my chest, and she returns the gesture as she tips up her chin.

"Nope. Celeste needed my help."

The woman in question rounds the doorframe, clearing her throat.

I spin back to find her lips pursed together.

Oh, I see how it is.

My kid and the woman who can barely stand me are . . . teaming up on me?

"This true? Or did you just lure her here with cookies to mess with me, Celeste?"

It's the first time I've called her by her first name, and her expression morphs from nonchalant to surprise before she has time to school it back. When my brows fall along with my patience, I turn back.

A hand catches my biceps. "No, it's not her fault."

Now, my brows are raised, my gaze falling to the fine hand that barely wraps halfway around my arm.

"Sorry, it was my fault. And for what it's worth, Maisey *was* helping me."

There's a beat that passes between us before she realizes

her hand still grips my arm. When her fingers fall away, I glance between her and Maisey.

"I'll see you at home in ten." I give her my best dad-means-business face, and she nods, her mouth full of cookie and the glass gripped in her small hand.

"Sorry for scaring you, Daddy," Maise says after swallowing the cookie down with a sip of milk.

I grunt and shake my head.

A parent's worst nightmare is losing a kid. At least, it's mine. Maise is my damn life. And I hers, whether it should be that way or not.

"I'll walk her home," Celeste says with a shy smile.

"You sure you can cross over into enemy territory and live to tell the tale?" I grind out, walking past her, my shoulder brushing hers.

I ignore the heat that lances with the tiniest of contact.

"I'll stick it out. For Maisey."

I huff a low sound that's pure sarcasm with maybe a hint of amusement. *Sure she will.*

But the woman takes care of her father, which is no easy feat. And from all the stories I've heard in our short time here, both Hank and his family were the heart and soul of Grafton for a long time. Before they left for one reason or another.

I let the screen door slam behind me and trudge through the half-melted tide of snow back to the house. Maisey is good with people, and if she needs to come home, she will.

And besides, I can pretty much see them from my kitchen window. On that note, I find doing dishes more appealing than I should. Running water into the sink, I add dish detergent before swirling the hot water with my hand.

Over the snow-covered white picket fence, I see Maise and Celeste move about the kitchen. They huddle by the oven, peering into it like they're looking for damn treasure . . .

When Celeste opens the door and Maisey hands her an oven mitt, she slides out whatever they were looking at and turns, dropping it on the counter.

It's not marble.

Maisey's hands flail in the air. She's telling Celeste something very animatedly.

The pan comes up, a tea towel slides underneath it as she sets it back down. They stand back as if admiring whatever is in that pan.

And then I see it . . .

Maisey, my only child and best little bud, holds her hand high. Our thing. The way we celebrate, well, *everything*.

Celeste slaps hers to it and they jump around celebrating who knows what.

Something like envy or annoyance snaps in my chest. I growl at the selfish sentiment. A girl needs friends apart from just her old man. *Especially* someone who isn't her old man.

With her mother nonexistent in our life, she could use

someone who understands the things she will go through. Girl stuff.

I always thought I would find someone to share our life with before she got to that point. Guess there's still time . . .

The washing up is done in a few minutes. And I busy myself with business, lining up next month's jobs for the crew and replying to the never-ending emails that insist on pouring in, despite the holidays coming up.

It takes a solid hour to get through it all. And when I look up from the laptop, the sky is dark outside.

Dammit.

I push from the chair, stretching. The house is far too quiet. Maisey still isn't home. Walking to the front door, I put on my coat and walk outside. I pull the door closed behind me and hear raucous laughter a second later.

The Blacks' house is lit up, the happy sounds of Maise and her new friend spilling from somewhere behind the huge old home. I take the side gate and make my way down to the backyard. Flood lights hanging from the eaves light up the glittering winter snow that's still coating every inch of Hank's yard.

Hank himself is bundled up and sitting on a lawn chair among the snow as Maisey runs around, scooping up snow as she goes, rolling it into a ball. She ducks behind one of the few trees. I cross the snow to stand beside Hank.

"Evening," I offer.

He looks up from his book, Mark Twain something or other.

"Oh, hi there. Have a seat."

I chuckle, noticing there isn't another seat besides the one he's sitting in. When his stare doesn't leave my face, I nod toward the back of the house. "I'll just go grab one."

I pop into the sunroom and take a chair from by the back door. He must store them away in case of blizzards and such.

I plop the chair by him and drop into it.

It's cold out here, but he doesn't seem to mind as he scans the yard without another word.

"Who are you looking for?" I ask.

The smile that lights up his face warms my chest. "Tisha, she's hiding from me."

Tisha?

I clear my throat. I know his condition is pretty bad, but I thought his immediate family would, you know, stick?

"You know where she'd run off to?" I prompt.

"She's good at this game. But I'll get her soon enough."

Utterly perplexed, I can't peel my gaze from his face.

Something hard and wet smacks into the side of my head. A gasp follows with a curse.

Maisey is giggling like a damn fool as I lean and shake my head, dislodging the snow from my face.

"Oh my god, I am so sorry! I didn't realize you were here." Celeste's face is stretched under awkward regret.

"Tisha!" Hank perks up. "See, told you she'd find us."

Celeste's expression flattens before she schools it into a smile.

Geez, that must be tough. And for the first time since this hot-headed, ridiculous woman came into my life, I feel for her.

And the way Hank looks at her makes me wonder if she resembles whoever Tisha is.

I'm sure that's it. A good resemblance. Easy enough to mistake someone, especially in Hank's condition . . . I stand and pluck up the chair, planning on returning it.

"Please, can we stay just a little longer, Daddy?" Maisey runs for me, hanging from the chair in my hand. My cue to return it to the snowy ground from whence it came.

"It's late, kiddo. Maybe another time."

"Oh shoot, it is, too. Da—Hank, you need your dinner and meds." Celeste closes in on her father, helping him up from the chair.

"Sorry for keeping her," she adds as she brushes her father down with a hand while his gaze wanders the back-yard. She slips the book from his hand and closes it, tucking it under her arm.

"It's fine. I'm glad you guys had fun." The words are half defeat, half compassion. And fully feeling out of place coming from my lips. But the sentiment is genuine. I know exactly how exhausting being someone's full-time caretaker is. Being a single parent is not too different to what she's undertaking here. But at least Maisey is of sound mind and body. More than I can say for Hank.

Celeste has her hands full. And I daresay her heart, too.

"Well, we better be getting inside. Routine is every-thing." She forces a smile and leads her father back inside.

A heavy weight hangs on my free hand. "Daddy, can I come back tomorrow, after school? Pleeeeaaasseeee."

"I don't know, honey, I think Celeste has enough on her plate with Hank."

"Isn't he her daddy?" Her bright eyes reflect confusion.

"Yeah, he is. But Celeste takes care of him now."

"Oh, why? Aren't Daddies supposed to take care of their little girls, instead?"

"They are. But sometimes they need help, too."

"Oh," she huffs and starts for the side of the house, drag-ging me behind. "When will you need me?"

I chuckle. Walked right into that one.

"Maybe one day. Nothing to worry about now."

By the time we make it home and inside, I see Celeste cleaning up in the kitchen. Most of their lights are now out, the upper windows darkened. We eat a small meal of left-overs and Maisey helps me clean up. I run her a bath before tucking her into bed.

When I finally retire to my own room, I notice a window brightened on our side of the Black's house. Tugging my shirt off, I stare at it, wondering who's roo—

Celeste walks past in what looks like winter flannel paja-mas, twisting her hair with her hands and piling it on top of her head. She secures it with a clip before dropping onto the bed and pointing a remote at what I assume is the television mounted on the wall opposite the big bed.

Fuck.

I shouldn't be peering through the windows at her.

She taps the remote over and over before tossing it on the bed and picking up a book from her bedside.

I pad to my bathroom and shower before brushing my teeth and pulling on a T-shirt and boxers. Never seen the point of pajamas, really.

When I make it back to the bed, the light next door is still on.

I make a point to not look at it. Temptation proving stronger than I anticipated, I decide to check on Maise one last time. That way I'm out of line of sight of the window.

Padding across the hall, I push Maisey's bedroom door open a crack. She's sound asleep, still tucked in tight.

Perfect.

Sweet dreams, my girl.

En route to my room, I cross the threshold and close my door nearly all the way. Just leaving a few inches open so I can hear Maise.

Yawning, I cross the room to my side of the bed, the window side.

Celeste is still reading, her body relaxed against the headboard, her chest . . .

Holy shit.

My mouth goes dry instantly.

We may be dozens of feet apart, but there is no mistaking her hand as it travels the rounds of her chest. Her lips part as her head falls back. My shins hit the window seat, hands gripping the window frame as the air in my lungs turns to ash at the sight.

A beat later that same hand disappears into her pajama pants, and I swear I hear the moan through both sets of double-paned glass and across the distance between us.

Every inch of me wakes up as I watch her unravel.

Goddamn it.

CHAPTER

NINE

CELESTE

So this is my new 'project.'

The elementary school's Christmas play. My job is the backdrop artwork. And with just under two weeks until the twenty-fourth and the big show, I'm feeling the pressure. Luckily, I have been assigned someone to help build the set and put in some creative hours to help out.

If only they would turn up.

Apparently, they're a new family here. The dad was roped into this just as much as I was.

Poor guy is probably procrastinating. I know I was.

"Morning," a low voice says before clearing his throat.

I spin around and—

Oh great.

"Good morning," I say, feigning a happy tone.

Brilliant. The guy who barely tolerates my existence, except for when I'm entertaining his daughter.

Quinton.

"Sorry I'm late, Maise had a—"

I hold up a hand. "It's fine. Let's get to work."

We stand in the gymnasium's oversized open area, where art supplies and lumber are piled in their respective areas. My side is filled with large canvas tarps that are waiting to be muralled into an inch of their fraying edges and the other side . . . well, that is supposed to become the large frame to hang said mural backdrops from.

And we need a plan.

I will not be responsible for messing this up and wasting the school's limited resources. If there is one thing I take seriously in my life, it's art.

Someone has to.

It's only the sole expression of our existence on this planet as a species, after all.

No biggie.

Not to mention this is for the children's holiday play. Safe to say, the stakes are high.

"Where do you want these, love?" Dad wanders over with a container that he's . . . mixed all the paints together in.

Shit.

"Um—"

"Hank, good to see you again. You free to help with this

frame up?" Quinton asks, shooting me an empathetic look as his gaze sweeps over the mixed paint.

"Oh, Quin! Thought you'd never ask." Dad shoves the brown soupy mess into my arms and nods with a smile like he's just passed me over for men's business as he follows Quinton toward the pile of lumber. Maybe he will have better luck with something hands-on and not artistic?

And did he just call him *Quin*?

Now I feel like the third wheel . . .

"Daddy, where do you want these?" Maisey walks in, a tool belt in one hand, a tray of three coffees in the other.

Okay, make that the fourth wheel.

"Hi Celeste!" Maisey hands the tray to her dad, who has returned to where I stand as I gawk at his daughter. Her five years are seemingly more capable than my thirty. It's not every day you get showed up by a preschooler.

"Thanks, kiddo. Coffee, Celeste?" Quinton plucks a cup from the tray and hands it to me.

I stare at it like it's a cobra, not a cappuccino.

"Not a fan of caffeine?" he asks, his eyes narrowing with amusement.

I take the cup from his hand, my fingers brushing over his. "I like caffeine just fine, MacKelvie. Just not the kind that comes with strings."

"Strings?" His brows lower as he glances at his daughter.

I wait for Maisey to walk over to my father before saying, "You don't need to butter me up. I can be professional about this circumstance."

"I was—"

"Daddy, Hank says he doesn't drink whiskey in daylight hours?" Maisey is staring at my father who is walking the length of the timber pile, his hands on his hips.

"He doesn't, hey? Well, maybe Miss Francis would like one. I saw her in the hall when we got here," Quinton says.

Maisey screws her face up but wanders from the gymnasium to find who I assume is her teacher.

"Actually," I say, breaking his concentration from staring at the retreating back of his daughter. "Hank can't have coffee. Not anymore."

"Oh, damn, sorry. Noted." He runs a hand through his hair, and . . . that awkward silence hangs between us again.

"Right. I'm going to make a start. You good?" I wave a hand toward the timber and my father.

"Yep." Quinton buckles his tool belt around his waist as he glances to my dad. "Anything I need to know before we start?"

"About?"

"Your dad? The project?"

Huh. Look at us having a civil conversation that doesn't involve Maisey.

"No, not really. He was a capable man before . . . I'm sure this will be great for him."

"I'll do my best to keep up, then." He shoots me a smirk before walking over, slapping a hand on my father's shoulder. "Ready to get your hands dirty, Hank?"

"Dying to, son."

I can't take my eyes off them both. It's like giving my father something he's done for his whole life was the key to keeping him in the here and now.

All of our fussing and trying to keep him safe at home feels like the exact opposite of what he needs.

I huff a shocked breath and turn back to the rolls of canvas and container of brown paint. Which is kind of useless for the images the play director has requested. Damn, I'm going to have to go and get more.

"Quinton?" I call across the gym space.

"Yeah?" He turns back, sliding a carpenter's pencil behind his ear as his gaze finds me.

"I need more paints. You two okay here?"

"Course. Take your time."

He turns back, hands moving as he explains what he needs my father to do. Who, right now, is enraptured in the task he is getting the rundown on.

I pick up my bag and slide it over my shoulder, sipping the coffee Maisey brought in as I walk from the gym and head back to the truck.

Outside, snow is falling in short, gentle bursts. The street that the school is on is glistening with the white assault.

I start up the truck and head for the Village Store. The one-stop shop for all things in Grafton. Always has been.

I find a parking spot and swing the truck into it. Killing the engine, I slip inside.

"Morning, Celeste. Hear you're busy with the artistic

endeavors for the school play." Mr. Nolan winks at me like he has my entire life, every damn time I've stepped foot inside his shop. I think he thinks it's friendly.

I have news for him.

Mrs. Nolan pops out of an aisle with an armful of cereal boxes. "Oh! CC, I thought that sounded like you. How are you, darling?"

I chuckle. Now Mrs. Nolan, I like.

"I'm good, here let me help you with those."

I take half the pile of boxes precariously perched in her arms into my own.

"Thank you, sweetheart. Tell me, you met that new neighbor of yours yet?" Her eyes are lit up as she smiles over the remaining boxes in her hold.

"Yes, and don't go getting any ideas."

She laughs, so hearty it makes something small and light and happy tumble through my own lips.

"Oh, I would never." She rounds the counter and places the boxes on one end where a half-price ticket is taped to the front of the counter. I narrow my gaze at her and help her stack the boxes in their groups.

"Thanks, hon. But I'm guessing you didn't come in to help me rearrange the cereal. What are you chasing?"

"Tempera paint. Primary colors should be good enough."

"You out already? The art department only collected the supplies for the play last week." Despite the confusion wrapped around her face, she wanders to the aisle where the paints sit and hands me large bottles of red, yellow, and blue.

"There was an incident, and we now have one large supply of brown."

She giggles, but it fades when my face hasn't lit with amusement.

"Oh, sorry. Hank okay?"

"Yeah, the same can't be said for the paints. I'll pay for this lot."

"No, you won't. Consider this our contribution to the Christmas play."

"Thank you," I say softly, taking in her expression. There's empathy, but not sympathy. Maybe this small-town thing isn't so bad, after all . . .

I'm back at the school gymnasium before long and I haul the paint bottles in the crate that Mrs. Nolan lent me. When my father sees me carrying the heavy load, he skips out on the measuring he's doing, taking one end of the crate. We set it down on the floor by the rolled-up canvas backdrop material.

"You good here, miss?" he says.

Letting the smile that I ensure is plastered over my face stretch my features, I nod. "Yes, thank you, Hank."

A sheepish smile grows on his own face.

And I can just tell, all he is seeing at this moment is my mother. Who could blame him? She was an incredible human being.

A small hand slips into mine and I startle, turning to

find Maisey. She looks up at me. Her face is wrapped in sympathy when she whispers, "I promise I won't forget you, CC."

Just like that, emotion fills my throat like frostbit maple syrup. Slow and unrelenting in its onslaught.

She called me CC . . .

Wonder which one of the people I grew up among told her about that nickname. Probably Marie.

"Thanks, lovely." I scrunch my face, fighting back the burn behind my eyes and offer her a sad smile.

She takes off toward her dad, skipping as she waves her hands around. "CC thinks I'm lovely!"

Quinton spins back, a brow arched. "That so, kiddo?"

But his gaze isn't on his daughter now, it's planted on me as I stand and dwell in two very different warring feelings. Happiness and sadness. Although those words are too basic to describe what I feel right now.

"Give us a hand to set this frame out, hey?" he says, and she settles instantly, all business like her dad. She picks up a triangle-shaped tool and walks to the opposite end of the timber laying at Quinton's feet. Next to my father, she starts chatting away, bending down to adjust the wood. The triangle tool clatters to the floor, and she pushes it into the right angle she's made with the two lengths.

"Square!" she calls.

My father bends down after receiving the nod from Quinton, nailing the timber together with a thwack from the power tool in his hand. Is that a nail gun?

Oh my god . . .

A little anxious, I decide to trust Quinton's call and go about my large mural scene on this first canvas. I outline the image with a carpenter's pencil I manage to steal from the team on the other side of the gymnasium and slide it behind my ear when I'm done.

I hash out the background colors before starting the next canvas. Deciding to attack this large project in layers. Adding the finer details that make it at the very end.

Hours pass before I surface for a breather.

I find my father happy and sitting with Quinton and Maisey, eating . . . is that a sandwich?

Would you look at that.

No complicated menu here. Just hard work and simple food that comes with something that looks suspiciously like happiness.

And as a hearty laugh spills from my dad's throat at a story Quinton is animatedly telling with exaggerated hand gestures, I hug my arms around my body.

Why has this felt so hard? Until now.

I decide I've done enough for one day and mosey on over to where they sit. "How's the frame coming along?"

I slide my hands in the back pockets of my jeans, tugging my bottom lip through my teeth. All three look up, and Maisey jumps up, grabbing my hand. She maneuvers me between her and her dad and insists I sit.

I do, and my own father greets me like it's the first time we've met.

Quinton tilts his head toward me. "Hungry?"

"Starving, actually. I was going to go and grab something soon."

"We made enough for everyone, CC." Maisey hands me a wrapped-up sandwich.

"Oh, thank you. That's so sweet."

"Making progress with the backdrop?" Dad asks.

"Yes, the background elements are done. I'll work on the foreground tomorrow."

"Your art is important to you, isn't it?" my father asks, like he doesn't know me from the next stranger on the street.

"It is. Very much."

"How long you been painting?" Quinton asks.

I blow out a puffy breath. "A while."

"Is that what you were doing in the city?" Maisey asks.

I smile at her. "Yeah. At least, I was trying to."

Her brows fall. "What do you mean?"

"My work never really took off, not like my mother's did."

"She was an artist, too?" my father asks.

A pregnant pause passes, causing something in my chest to rise and burst. "She was."

My father stares at me, something like understanding passing through his gaze before he returns to his sandwich, washing it down with a sip from the bottle of water I assume Quinton supplied him with also.

"Well, I have actual work to get to. You good here?" Quinton says.

We all finish up and pack away the impromptu picnic.

"Great. Guess I'll see you tomorrow," I utter.

He closes in as I make to leave to follow my father who has wandered off. "Just one more thing."

I look into his eyes, lost as to what he could want.

His hand rises, sweeping past my ear, brushing my hair as his hand drops . . .

The stolen carpenter's pencil between his fingers.

"That's mine."

Oh shit, I momentarily forgot I had stolen it from his toolbox.

"I'm sorry, I would have returned it . . ." When I remembered I had it. Probably when I went for a shower and saw it in the mirror. God, I forgot it was even still there.

He chuckles.

"Any excuse to cross the boundary fence, neighbor." He adds a wink, and my face twists in shock.

Ah! Whatever, you ass. Where is the kind-hearted guy who took care of my confused father while I painted for the last three hours?

I find said father and usher him to the parking lot. When I have him bundled up in the truck, I round the front and climb into the driver's seat. I drop my head to the steering wheel as I replay the last moment I spent with Quinton MacKelvie. And to be honest, my father is not the only one confused in this truck.

Just when I thought he was tolerable, maybe even a nice guy, he goes and says something stupid.

Groaning, I fire up the truck.

"Where are we going?" Dad asks, snapping me back to reality.

"Home."

"Sure, sweetheart, let's go home."

Huh. A sliver of hope sparkles to life like the sunlight shimmering on the snow outside.

I'll take it.

CHAPTER

TEN

QUINTON

"You coming to the tree lighting in the square?" Caleb asks, shutting down the sander in his hand. It scuffs along the hardwood as it dies out.

"When?" I ask, slipping my dust mask up over my face.

"Tomorrow night."

"The school play is the week after. There's also sleigh rides. Is there any Christmas event this town doesn't do?"

Caleb chuckles. "Nope, not one."

I groan and start up a small palm sander. But who am I kidding, Maise is going to love this town. Christmas is her favorite holiday. She absolutely gets into every Christmas event or tradition she can. This afternoon, we have to hang decorations over the house. This weekend, she has penciled in hanging the lights on the porch and in the yard. And after the last three years of doing this, we have accumulated a

99

good amount of oversized Christmas-themed light-up yard decorations.

Hope the fuses hold out with all the extra power being pulled on the old house's system. Or the whole thing will be over before we can even light the first row of string lights.

We make short work of the last railing in the dining area of the inn before cleaning up the mess of fine dust and starting the wood treatment. A dark stain and varnish are what the owners wanted. So that's what they are getting. And even with the first coat, it looks stellar.

Caleb and I finish in an hour with the railing, moving onto the wainscoting installation. A new addition to the space, and frankly I think it makes the room. Success is in the details when it comes to a build, and it's another great choice. The room's facelift is looking incredible already, and we're only just past the halfway mark. We still have the rest of the column details to complete, and corbels in every doorway will add the finishing touches that make it shine.

Just in time for Christmas.

"So, you coming?" Caleb asks, pulling his mask down, his dark hair ruffled, his brown eyes homed in on me.

"Yeah, guessing so."

"Bringing CC?"

"Hey what?"

"Well, if you believe the latest on the Grafton grapevine, you two are quite the item. Playing happy families with Maisey and Hank."

"Shit. Who the hell told you that?"

He chuckles. "So not a thing, then? Asking for a friend."

"Yeah right, bud. And no, we're not a thing."

But the words don't fit right. Because even though they are the truth, I've started thinking about Celeste Black as more than just the girl next door. The woman who drives me crazy in every way she shouldn't.

And does she . . .

That's too soon, right?

We've barely had a handful of interactions.

But they were—intense.

No, that's stupid. I'm overthinking this. Like I do with most of the women I've been involved with.

Aren't I?

"Dude, you look like you're in pain. Your secret's safe with me. And I'll consider her out-of-bounds." Caleb slaps my shoulder and goes back to work. My face falls from whatever was twisting it up into an expression of surprise.

How is it everyone bar me has this shit figured out. Hell, Maise picks up on this stuff better than I do.

We finish the work for the day, and I swing past and pick up Maisey from school. She's got a few days left 'til the holidays, and she is literally counting down. She's elated when she climbs on up into the truck.

"I saw CC today." Her face beams at the mention of our new neighbor.

Oh no, she's got it worse than me.

"Was she working on the play backdrops?"

"I think so. But she gave us a talk on art and stuff after lunch. All the kids loved her."

"Right."

"Can we invite her over for dinner? Her daddy, too?"

"I don't know, Maise." I grind my jaw shut.

She's giving me the pleading prayer hands, her eyes puppy-wide as she blinks like that will enhance her cuteness to a level I won't be able to resist.

I sigh. "Fine. But you're helping me cook."

"Yes!" She fist pumps the air.

"And . . ." I say with a low tone, much like a warning. "It's still a school night, little miss. No staying up late and conning Celeste and Hank into staying later."

"Okay, Daddy. Geez, you don't have to repeat everything to me all the time."

"Just getting in first. I don't want you to forget conveniently."

She screws up her face as we pull into our driveway.

"Right, chores and then we can plan dinner."

"Should I go over and invite them first?" she asks.

"Sure, kiddo. But straight back home, you hear?"

"Fine."

She's out the door before I have a chance to kill the engine. I shake my head with a low chuckle. Guess there's no getting out of seeing Celeste—not anymore, now that Maise has her sights on being her friend. Whether the woman wants a five-year-old bestie or not.

"Pass the potatoes, will you, Tisha?" Hank says.

Celeste picks up the large porcelain bowl and hands it to him with a smile plastered on her face. How she keeps it together when the man who raised her has long forgotten her, I'll never know. She's braver than she gives herself credit for. Braver than most people, who would simply stick Hank in a home and move on with their lives.

"Mr. Black, you've lived here for like a century, right? What was it like?" Maise asks.

For a second, I panic, thinking Celeste is going to intercept. Wishing my daughter wasn't so damn curious.

"Well, I'm not that old. But I guess it was much the same. Although, if I remember rightly, the woman who lived here before you was nowhere as pretty as you." He gives her a cheeky smile and then, "I wonder where she went..."

"Probably moved, Hank. How's those potatoes?" Celeste asks.

So, they're not telling him my grandmother died?

Why?

Not wanting to be the one to spill the beans, I help shift the subject to something lighter. "You're good with your hands, Hank. Thanks for helping out today. Would have been in a real pickle without you."

He nods, delight flooding his features. "Any time."

"Yes, I was meaning to thank you for that." Celeste meets my gaze, and I'm pretty sure we're not talking about the backdrop frame anymore.

"Nah, all good."

Hank's focus ping-pongs between us.

I cut into my steak and load up some green vegetables onto it before shoveling it into my mouth, lest I say something stupid. Like, *any excuse to be near you*, or maybe . . . *what book are you reading at the moment? You know, the one-handed read you—*

I swallow, clearing my throat, trying to usher that last thought out of my mind.

"I'm done," Maise chirps, her cutlery dropping into the center of her plate.

She most certainly is not. A pile of vegetables sits to one side of her plate, her meat half eaten.

"Half those vegetables, young lady, and three more bites of your steak."

"Argh, Daddy, no. I want to play with CC." She jiggles in her seat.

Surprise fills Celeste's eyes as she sets her cutlery down. Her plate is almost cleared.

"Maise," I warn.

"No, it's okay," Celeste says softly. "I've been needing some girl time for ages."

Maisey is practically pinging off her chair. Lips pursed, hands steepled in her pleading prayer pose.

Good Lord, this girl lays it on thick.

"Fine, two more bites of each. Not negotiable."

She snatches up her fork, shoveling in all four bites at once, and chews with blown-out cheeks as she wiggles on her chair.

Celeste simply watches her with an amused expression.

When my daughter swallows dramatically and flies from her chair, she grabs Celeste's hand, almost pulling her over as she tries to rise from the table in a flurry of limbs. But to Celeste's credit, she chuckles and follows willingly.

"More potatoes, Hank?"

"No thanks, this old man is full." He leans back in his chair, and we chat about vague things like the weather, how the season is tracking this year, and the old houses we live in. Not once in the ten minutes we spend together does he refer to his daughter. Only his wife gets a mention when he recounts one particularly cold winter, that from what I gather was over twenty years ago.

When footsteps thunder back downstairs, I go to intercept Maisey before she can rope Celeste into a damn sleepover or something of the sorts.

"Mai—"

I slam into fragrant softness, dark hair tumbling over her shoulders and into my chest.

Not Maisey.

"Oh, shit, sorry," Celeste breathes.

I steady her with my hands firmly on her arms. Her dark eyes flick up to my gaze. Her last breath stutters out as her eyes darken, the pupils swallowing the dark cinnamon color that sparkles under Maisey's deluge of Christmas lights.

"Don't be," I utter. "You all good?" I step back, releasing my grip.

A shaky smile ghosts over her lips. "Yup."

"Don't let Maise con you into anything you don't want to do."

"I'm afraid that ship has sailed."

I tilt my head, waiting for her to elaborate.

"No, not Maisey, she's wonderful. I was just referring to my life in general."

And there it is—the statement that speaks volumes as to how she feels about being back here. At least, that's my assumption.

"Tell you what, how about you help me with the dishes, and I'll listen."

She goes to object, and I close in again.

"I'm a pretty good listener, Celeste."

Too close.

I'm too close. She's all elegant angles and curves. Smells fucking edible, and when her bottom lip disappears between her teeth, hell, I have to check myself.

Finally, she says, "Okay. Maybe the abridged version, since it's getting late."

"Perfect."

I reroute to the dining room and collect the plates.

Hank has wandered to the living room and is browsing the bookshelf. In the kitchen, I find Celeste adding soap to the water in the sink, her hand dipping into it as she swirls the suds to life.

And the pure domesticity of this moment steals a breath, holding it hostage before I can wrangle another in. When my brain flickers back online, I place the dishes to her right and swipe up a tea towel from the oven handle.

"Sorry, I hope it's okay that I wash?" she says softly.

"Go for it."

She washes as I dry, and we settle into a comfortable silence before she breaks it. "Thanks for feeding my father and me."

"It was our pleasure. And it was Maisey's idea."

She chuckles. "I believe it."

"She really likes you."

"Ditto." She looks at me with a soft expression as she rinses a plate and places it on the drying rack. "Oh, look at that, you can see right into our kitchen window from yours."

That's not the only set of windows that line up between our two houses. But I keep that to myself, not willing to admit I've seen her through my bedroom window. Out of shame—at least, that's what I tell myself.

"So, I'm all ears."

"Ah. Well, I am the youngest of three. And the only one without a career, so I drew the short straw and had to come home for our father."

"I see. What do your siblings do?"

"One older brother, thirty-five, and an older sister who is thirty-two. Both corporate, Ben's a lawyer and Hannah is in real estate. Safe to say they weren't going to leave their jobs for Dad."

"So that makes you the kind one?"

She huffs a strained laugh. "More like the useless one."

"Celeste," I say, my tone low and lined with annoyance. This woman is many things, useless is not one of them.

"I'm self-aware enough to be able to admit when I have nothing to show for the last decade, Quinton."

She returns to the washing up, her movements becoming more rigorous with every swirl of the suds-soaked cloth. And when her cheeks redden and she doesn't look up from her task, I can guess where her thoughts are at.

"Hey," I say, resting my hand on her wrist to still it. "Don't do that to yourself."

She swallows and eventually turns her head to meet my gaze. And fuck, hers is silver lined.

Sniffing, she attempts to dry her eyes with her sleeve at the crook of her elbow.

Dammit.

I never intended for my listening to end like this.

A crash rings out from the living room.

"Oh shit. Dad." Celeste is peeling away from the sink, drying her hands on her jeans as she rushes from the kitchen toward the sound.

ELEVEN

CELESTE

"Da—Hank, are you okay?" I drop to my knees by the shelf of records that's been knocked over, the vinyls spread over the hardwoods.

"Ah, I'm fine." He bats my hand away and pushes up off the floor, first onto all fours then to his feet.

What on earth was he doing?

"Sorry 'bout all this, Quin. I was just looking at your artwork. Guess I lost my balance."

It's now that I see a large landscape hanging over where the shelf was against the wall of the living room.

"I can clean it up." Bending down, I gather the records as Quinton rights the shelf, returning it to its place against the wall.

"Tisha," Dad says, excitement lining his voice, "hell, this is one of yours!"

I snap my gaze up, and finally I see the tiny scrawl of

mom's signature in the bottom right corner. A Tisha Black original, by the looks of it. Mrs. MacKelvie must have bought it from her all those years ago.

"So it is." I stand and come to stare up at the painting as my father is doing.

Dad gives me a curious look, as if I'm the one who's lost their mind, not recognizing my own work. Except it's not my work. My art pales in comparison to my mother's. Always has. Her oil paintings were incredible, with depth and detail I've never been able to achieve.

And that is the sole reason I haven't stepped foot in her art studio at the back of our yard since the day she died. Twenty-three years. And I've not seen a single work of hers apart from the few in our house and now this one.

"How long ago was it when you did this one?" Dad asks before turning to Quinton. "You've got good taste, man."

It's been so long since I've thought about my mother's work in any practical sense. Her style and talent were her gift, and she was happy to share it with the world. Much like Maisey has, apparently, shared her love of Christmas with the world. This house is absolutely dripping with green and red festivities. It's hard to find a surface not decorated.

The grinch in me wants to cringe at the vibrant display of happiness.

"CC! Are you coming back?" an impatient voice drifts down the stairwell.

Speak of the—

"Manners, Maise!" Quinton calls up the staircase.

I tamp back the grin that wants out over my face. He's just like every other parent I've met—overprotective, trying his best to install manners into his daughter despite her rebellious streak.

"It's fine, I should get up there." I glance between Dad and Quinton.

"Yeah, sure, we could use a whiskey in the cigar room, couldn't we, Hank?" Quinton chuckles.

Ah, secret men's business.

I know my cue . . .

I take the stairs two at a time back up to the bedroom Maisey has decorated with her own touch, including an overload of Christmas cheer. I knock softly on the wall by her doorframe. She jumps off the bed, scooting my way. Grabbing my hand, she tugs me inside and swings the door closed.

"What took you so long? I thought my dad stole you away from me."

She's frowning, all pouty and cute.

"No, he didn't. But I did help a little. It's the right thing to do when you're a guest."

"Sure. But he can do it, you know. He just likes the company."

I bet he does.

It must be lonely raising a kid on your own.

Much like caring for an ailing parent on your own, I guess.

"Want to play hairdressers and do our makeup? I made

Daddy buy me a makeup kit. It's really cool."

She rushes to her dresser and returns with a pink plastic makeup case. Through the clear lid, I see bright pinks, outrageous blue eye shadow, sparkly lip gloss, and something that looks like neon-pink blush.

Dear Lord.

"Sure, you want me to do yours first?"

"Nah, Daddy will make me wash it off for bedtime. But I can do yours!"

"Oh, I—"

She makes something that looks like puppy dog eyes at me and pleads with her small hands pressed together.

"Fine, okay. But if I end up looking like a clown—I mean—just take it easy. My dad's going to make me wash mine off, too . . ."

She giggles and manhandles me onto the edge of the bed. I sit as she shifts behind me and quickly wraps my hair up before adding a claw clip. Half of my hair falls from it, but she doesn't seem to notice as she instructs me to stay still.

Maisey drags her dresser chair close to me and stands on it. The palate lands in my hands and she gets to work. I close my eyes, letting the light touch of her brush drift over my face. Her soft fingertips graze my skin occasionally, reminding me how little she is.

She's adorable.

Feisty and independent.

I love that for her.

I wish I had more Maisey in me and less . . . CC?

A girl could learn a lot from this little lady, as my dad calls her.

When I'm all done, she holds a mirror up to my face.

And I absolutely look like a drag queen.

I clear my throat and turn my head side to side as if assessing her makeup skills. "Brilliant, thank you."

"You really like it?" I swear she's holding her breath.

"I do."

"We should show Daddy."

"Oh, oh no. Maybe—"

"Daddy!"

She's off the stool and out the door a heartbeat later.

There's nothing left to do but laugh. Maybe Maisey's Christmas cheer is rubbing off on me, after all.

So I decide to run with it.

"You look pretty," Quinton says, barely keeping a straight face.

"Why thank you, Mr. MacKelvie." The words are loaded with sass, as if this is some 1920s black-and-white romance film from the Deep South. *Gone with the Wind* type stuff. I swing the tea towel over my shoulder for dramatic effect.

And god . . . I must look ridiculous.

His shoulders shake as he washes the last dish from the dessert we snuck in, secure in the knowledge that Maisey was sound asleep.

"How long you going to keep this new look?" he prompts.

"Well, I was thinking about heading down to the market, or maybe Maple Acres, you know. Might catch the attention of somebody special."

He doubles over, hands gripping the edge of the porcelain sink.

I can't help but laugh, too. When he comes up for air, his laughter petering out, tears stream down his face. "I'm sorry, it's just been a really long time since I laughed that hard."

My own laughter fades at that.

"In that case, you absolutely need a makeover, too." I give him a mock sympathetic look, pretending to assess the angles of his face, his jawline, his . . .

Deep blues catch my gaze. The corner of his mouth still tipped up, he swallows as it drops, his lips parting.

I want to . . .

I brush the pads of my fingers over his jawline. The angles that I've been noticing all night. I shouldn't be—

Quinton clears his throat.

I step out of his space, realizing too late that I wandered into his proximity.

"You want a baby wipe or a warm washcloth to take that

off?" His voice is low and all business. A stark contrast to the happy tone it was just seconds ago.

"Sure," I finally rasp out.

He pulls the plug in the sink and dries his hands before disappearing from the kitchen. I wander to the living room, finding my father snoring. He looks so content, peaceful.

And I just watch him for a moment, taking him in. Letting the seconds turn into a cluster of time, creating a new memory of my dad. It's bittersweet, knowing his peace will be lost when he opens his eyes. That this may be one of the last memories I make of him before the disease renders him too far gone.

Emotion clogs my throat, and I wrap my arms around myself, willing the morbid thoughts away.

"Hey," a soft baritone interrupts my sad state.

I turn to find Quinton, warm washcloth in the hand he has extended to me. But I can't bring myself to take it. Still fighting the reality of what's left of my last parent. Overcome with hurt and grief in the shape of another impending loss.

Tears burn as I meet his gaze.

"Celeste," he says softly.

A tear slips from the well lining my eyes, and I slam them shut.

Warmth, sandalwood, and spice surround me instantly. My face meets a hard wall of muscular chest.

Oh shit.

I chug a sob into the warm comfort he affords me. His

hand wraps around the back of my neck like we've been doing this our whole lives. The other hand is holding me to him like if he only holds tight, he can ward off whatever is causing me hurt.

He feels so . . . safe.

The loneliness I've been barely keeping at bay finally retreats far enough away that I can't feel its cold bite.

It's a relief. A grounding feeling I never knew I needed.

He swallows, and I feel his Adam's apple bob.

Shit, I'm lingering.

I push from his hold, drying my face, breathing through the last of the emotion. "I'm so sorry, I didn't mean to snot all over your shirt. Crap."

He doesn't look down, only releasing me from his hold gradually as if he can't let go until he's sure I'm okay.

No wonder his daughter is so incredible. She has the most amazing parent as a role model.

"Celeste, you don't have to do this alone."

"Says Mr. Single Parent."

Instantly, I know it was the wrong thing to say. But I've never been very good at tense moments. One of the reasons I could never hold a career, let alone a decent-paying job. "I—"

He waves a hand, shaking his head. "Forget it, I know what you mean. I'm not exactly over here asking for help, either. It's always just been me and Maise. I've never felt the need to ask. She's my kid, so I'll raise her, you know. My responsibility, not anyone else's. Besides, it's my privilege."

And . . . there goes my ovaries.

I huff a strained laugh, and he tilts his head, saying, "What?"

I work through a breathy chuckle. "Nothing, really."

"Well, Little Miss Nothing, you still have," he says, waving a hand in front of my face, "a cleanup job on your hands."

"Oh, yeah, sorry." I grab for the washcloth.

He doesn't relinquish it.

Instead, he moves in, tilting my face with a finger under my chin. "I got it."

Methodically, gently, he wipes away the gawdy makeup from my face. Taking his time, he moves over my cheeks, forehead and jaw.

"Close your eyes, CC," he rasps, shifting a little closer.

His warmth wakes up my body. The touch of his palm holding my face at an angle to help remove the makeup tingles, radiating through my jaw, down my neck, and straight to my chest.

My breathing shallows out as he turns the rag to use the corner and swipes it over my eyelids. One, then the other.

"Almost done," he says, voice like gravel.

No words form as my lips part. His grip reaffirms over my jaw as the cloth brushes over my bottom lip. And I swear the room just got a hundred degrees hotter.

Didn't it?

When the fabric meets my top lip, I can barely draw a useful breath.

I chug through each plummeting cycle as his touch sears through my skin. But the cloth disappears, as does his warmth, a beat later. "All done."

Eyes fluttering open, I feel like someone's sent my body through the wringer.

The cloth is still in his now white-knuckled grip.

"Qui—"

He's in my space again, the cloth falling from his hand as he palms my face. I search his gaze, his pupils now blown out, the blue almost swallowed by the darkness lingering in them our proximity has caused.

"I want to . . ." He tilts his head, closing his eyes briefly.

"Then do it," I rasp.

"You sur—"

"Celeste? Why'd you let me fall asleep?" My father pops up from the sofa, his face slackened by sleep, but his eyes holding a clarity I rarely see.

Quinton's hold falls away as he makes space between us, snapping his attention to Dad. "Had quite the nap there, Hank."

Dad rubs his hands over his face, confusion lining his gaze as he takes in Quinton and me standing by the sofa. And then, as if someone shuttered a filter over his gaze, his eyes all but glaze over. "Where am I?"

"Next door, we had dinner here. Remember, Da— Hank?" I say, shoving my hands into my back pockets.

"Oh, yes, so we did. Well, we better be getting home, Tish."

"Sure." I offer my hand, and he rises from the sofa.

"You okay? Your face looks funny," Dad says.

How do I answer that? Is it because I'm not his Tisha or because I just had a pound of neon makeup wiped from my face? Or is it because I almost kissed the handsome, sweet single dad next door?

And I really, really wanted to.

TWELVE

QUINTON

Fuck, she felt good.

So damn good. And I can't get the look that claimed her face out of my head as I lay awake at 11:55 p.m. Only a few hours later, and I am still hovering around that one singular moment we shared. I can't shake it.

It's been forever since a woman affected me.

And never like that, never with just a touch.

Dammit.

She was animated tonight. Happy. It's the first time I've seen her anything but focused, annoyed, or stressed-out.

And she was goddamn stunning.

Celeste's light is still on. But now I can't bring myself to peer through my window.

As much as I want to, I won't.

Can't.

My fingertips still hold the ghost of her touch. Her skin

so silky soft, her dark eyes burning with the same thing that was threatening to take me down. At least I think that's what it was for her, too.

I roll over, my tense body digging into the mattress. My mind latches onto one thing—touching Celeste—and fucking runs with it.

Cock impossibly hard, I rub my hands down my face with a groan.

I'm a fucking idiot, fantasizing over the woman next door. More complications are probably the last thing she wants. I'm probably the last man she wants, if our history is anything to go by.

But fuck me.

She's damn well edible.

So beautiful and sweet, the way she plays with Maise. Selfless, the way she cares for Hank . . .

Hell, I may as well get her out of my system. I grip my cock in one hand and pump. Every angle, elegant curve, and sound of Celeste floods back in.

Every stroke takes me higher, every image of her cementing her somewhere deep.

I shoot loads of ropey release over my boxers with a low moan.

But the high is fleeting. Shallow and soulless.

It doesn't abate the need, doesn't even take the edge off.

Well, shit.

Maisey drags me along behind her as we make our way through the snow to the town center for the Christmas tree lighting. Folks have already started drifting in from around town, and strategically placed speakers play holiday music with a comforting crackle. The stars overhead pale in comparison to the bright faces around us.

It's barely halfway through the month, but Grafton has Christmas in full swing. The tree lighting, apparently, is the official start to the long list of festivities. A few people say hello as I wander behind my daughter, snow crunching under my boots, the winter darkness kept at bay with the copious amounts of string lights and the lit-up Christmas displays in each storefront on Main Street.

"Hey Quinton, how's the inn coming along? Going to be ready for Christmas Day dinner? You know, my family has tables booked there," Jeffrey Stiles says, forcing a smile as if he's worried his plans are going to fall through.

"Sure thing, started on the finishes yesterday." I slap his shoulder, and he nods, muttering something that sounds like "great, great" as he turns away and disappears through the crowd.

People bustle around the enormous tree that stands

proudly in the center of the square. The small tug on my hand reminds me I'm supposed to be following.

"Coming, Maise."

"You're so slow. Stop talking to everyone, Daddy."

She weaves her way through the mass of bundled-up neighbors toward a handful of food stalls. We come to a stop in front of the candy stall. Of course we do.

I chuckle. "This is what you're killing yourself over, kiddo?"

"It's a once-a-year thing. You can't be too early. If they run out . . ." Her eyes narrow as she scans the rows of treats. I know what she's after. And when her shoulders slump and her face screws up, I know they're out.

Candy apples.

Not exactly a scarcity during the rest of the year, but her favorite nonetheless.

"Sorry, Maise. Pick something else, hey?"

She leans into my side. Now I'm kicking myself for not leaving work earlier and getting to the event sooner. The line we walk between putting food on the table and being parents is a fine, treacherous one some days.

My heart aches for her as she mutters, "Never mind, let's go find CC."

"Sure, sweetheart."

Making a mental note to find candy apples online and order a subscription later tonight that I can dole out throughout the year, I pick her up and place her on my hip.

She cuddles into me, and her little sniffles have my hand running over her hair as I wade through the happy folks.

A minute later, by the food van, we find CC ordering. Two guys stand just behind her.

I make my way over, Maise still pouting into my neck, not willing to face the happiness all around her in her saddened mood.

"Hey there," I offer.

"Oh, hi, Quinton." Celeste takes her food from the vendor.

She passes some to Hank, who has a large basket swinging from his arm by the handle, before turning to pass a burger and drink to Caleb.

The hell?

I study the interaction like it's some kind of hostage situation, not knowing who will survive. The intensity must register all over my face, because Celeste says, "Do you know Caleb, Quinton? We went to the same high school."

Caleb chuckles. "CC, Quinton is my new boss."

"Oh, sorry, I didn't realize." Her gaze widens as her cheeks flush, and I'm betting it's not from the cold.

"I won't keep you guys, then. Have a great night," I say.

If three is a crowd, then five is just plain awkward. But as I turn to leave, CC's gaze shifts to Maisey, still huddled and wrapped around my shoulder.

"Hey baby, what's going on?" CC says softly, her fingers brushing over Maisey's hair.

The gesture is so gentle, so maternal, it takes me aback. The naturalness of it all.

And on cue, my daughter pops her head up. Wiping away tears and snot onto her sleeve, she reaches for CC.

I relinquish my hold, and CC takes her, setting her on her feet and kneeling in front of her. "Tell me what's got this brilliant girl all upset." She brushes a damp strand of hair from Maisey's face behind her ear. I grind my jaw shut, not allowing the way my chest swells with their intimate interaction to show on my face.

"I wanted a candy apple, but when we got there," Maisey says with a sniffle, glancing up at me, "we were too late. They were all gone."

"Oh, baby. That's too bad. Your dad had to work a little later, did he?"

Maise simply nods, dropping me in it.

"Well, you know what? I was there earlier, and I bought some things." CC stands and takes the basket from Hank. "You take mine, sweetheart."

Celeste hands Maisey a candy apple, bright red and wrapped in transparent cellophane.

Maisey's eyes light up, rounding as she peers into the basket. There's a bunch of candy apples, cotton candy, and candy canes. "These are all for you?!"

"Me and you, but we have to eat them slowly." CC winks at her.

She bought half the damn stand. It's a shit ton of sugar.

Maisey flies into her arms, hugging her tight.

Celeste meets my gaze. "Before you say no outright, I planned on making these last all year. I wasn't sure which was her preference, so I got a few of everything."

I don't know what to say.

I don't know what has stolen my words . . .

The fact that Celeste plans on staying that long, or that she intends on spending it with Maisey.

Emotion thickens my airways, and I shift my gaze to the little girl still wrapped around the woman I can't get out of my head. Not since our almost kiss.

Caleb shuffles, pointing something out to Hank. And the moment is over.

"Come on, Maise, let's go see the tree lights." I extend a hand to her.

She still clings to Celeste. "I'm going to watch it with CC, Daddy. You can come if you want."

How generous, kiddo.

"Sure thing." I meet Celeste's gaze, and she smiles, assenting.

"You guys coming to watch the tree?" Celeste turns back, holding the basket out to Hank. He looks at it but walks off with Caleb, obviously forgetting the last few minutes.

With a soft sigh, Celeste adjusts the handle of the basket over her arm. She keeps checking on Hank as he moves through the crowd.

"Caleb won't let him wander off," I offer.

"I know. I still worry. Not everyone is used to needing eyes in the back of their heads to—"

Her head dips as she takes in my 'oh yeah' face.

"I guess you're the exception. You seem to have this parenting thing down, so . . ."

I chuckle at that. "No, Celeste. Nobody does. Sometimes we get lucky, and it just looks that way."

The music stops abruptly, and the speakers crackle before a whiny screech sails through them from a microphone somewhere. The town mayor steps up onto a rickety platform in front of the tree.

"Alright, folks. Welcome! Welcome to the annual Grafton Christmas tree lighting. We are so excited for the holiday season and all the fun it brings. So, without further delay, light her up!"

The crowd falls silent as a young boy bends down and flicks a switch at the base of the tree.

Rainbow hues of green, red, silver, and warm gold explode over every bough. Gasps rapture through the audience, cheers and applause growing as the mayor swings her arms toward the tree. "Merry Christmas, Grafton!"

"Merry Christmas!" the crowd chants back.

Kids run around, adults discuss holiday plans as they admire the tree, and happiness radiates from every single soul here.

All except one.

I take in the sorrow in Celeste's face as she raises her gaze, looking at the tree before us. "It's really beautiful." A heartbreaking contrast to the melancholy words that leave her lips.

"It is," I whisper.

When her eyes meet mine, her sadness tugs at my heart. How devastating to lose something that's supposed to be as special as the holidays to grief.

"Cele—"

"CC, think Hank's ready to head home." Caleb interrupts by cutting in between us, despite the closeness that rose during the light display. But when we look to where he's nodding, Celeste swears under her breath and takes off after her father. Currently peeling off his layers and shaking his head, he gets the attention of more and more of the crowd.

Dammit.

"Daddy, why's Mr. Black taking his clothes off? He'll catch cold," Maise says, hands coming to rest on her hips.

"He's just confused. CC will help him get home."

"Oh." The little sound is disappointment personified.

Squatting, I take her by the arms. "How about we head home, too? That way, if CC needs a hand later, you can help out."

"Can I stay up later than usual if I help?"

"Sure thing."

"Yes!" She jumps on the spot before strangling my neck with her arms.

I sweep her onto my hip. "Let's get out of this cold, hey?"

We head for the truck. And when we reach the parking lot, Celeste is helping her half-dressed dad into their truck. And it hits me . . .

In this stage of Hank's condition, Celeste is the parent. But unlike my relationship with my daughter, her happy moments are much rarer with Hank. Double that with the memories of the man and father he used to be, and that makes my heart hurt for her.

Hell, when did I turn into such a damn sap?

"Daddy, let me in?" Maise tilts her head at me, frowning.

"Yeah, let's go home." I unlock the truck and open the door before tucking her into her booster seat, securing her belt.

Closing the door, I glance back at Celeste. She's leaning on the passenger door, but her forehead is pressed against the glass. Defeat is written all over her face. And I decide in that moment to help her anyway I can.

Whether she wants my help or not.

She's turned her life upside down to take care of her father.

But who is looking after Celeste?

THIRTEEN

CELESTE

The house is bare. Compared to Quinton and Maisey's home, it feels dull. And for the first time in years, I feel the urge to decorate. To see this holiday, one that's caused our family nothing but hurt, in a different light. My phone lights up with an incoming call.

Marie.

"Hi! How are you?" I answer, sliding onto a kitchen stool.

"Celeste, it's so good to hear your voice. How are things going with your father?"

I pause to find something to say that doesn't sound like I'm barely holding this house together. Literally and figuratively. "It's going, I guess. I'm no cook, but I think he's fed and watered appropriately." I add a little chuckle to lighten the fact that I'm not great at this like Marie is.

"Oh hon, nobody expects you to be everything to everyone, everywhere. That's not what I was asking. Has he deteriorated any more since I left?"

I can hear the guilt in her voice.

And I do my best not to associate my part in this with the fact that Hank Black has, in fact, been having fewer lucid moments and has been more upset lately than I ever remember.

"He has, a little. I'm sorry."

"It's not your fault, sweetheart. Just the disease. Maybe I should come back?"

For a beat I desperately want her to.

But that's just another selfish thought. One I should be strong enough to tamp out.

"Nope. I've got this, Marie. You've spent enough time taking care of our family. I promise if things get tough, I'll find more help."

"Okay . . . you sure?"

The line stays silent for a moment before I set my shoulders back. "I'm sure. Enjoy your time. You've more than earned it."

"In that case, consider me your backup plan."

"I will. And Marie?"

"Yeah, hon?"

"Thank you for loving us," I say softly, the words strangled a little as my throat tightens.

"I made a promise to your mother, and I was happy to. Love you, hon."

"Love you, too."

The line goes dead, and I set my phone on the countertop. It's so good to hear her voice. Marie always felt like our second mother. And didn't that come with its own messed-up set of baggage? Which brings me back to the first thought I had before she rang.

This house looks lifeless.

I slip off the stool and wander around the big old home. And with every step I take, I notice more and more things that need maintenance or replacing. Dust covers every flat surface, and a few webs have bloomed in the archway leading to the corridor that meets the front door.

Right.

Well, if I'm going to own this new phase of my life and step up for my father and myself, this pity party I've been throwing myself ends now.

The cleanup phase starts this second. And maybe after I give every room and every corner of this old house the once-over, I can leave some baggage behind. Maybe even toss it out with some of the old crap I'm sure has been hoarded since Mom died.

When I reach the sunroom, I find Dad in his reading chair, asleep. Where he is more often than not. His routine is becoming more and more simple by the day, despite his needs increasing.

With him settled, I get to work. Rummaging through the kitchen cupboards, I grab large garbage bags and cleaning products. Rags and some polish, too.

I start on the living room, making my way around the

space. I leave the corner the tree sits in 'til last. The hardwood floor is littered with pine needles, fallen from the neglected tree. Another thing that needs some TLC. I sweep away the mess and water the tree. But somehow it still looks sad. I'm sure Maise would be annoyed with my lame decorating attempt. Maybe I can ask her for help bringing this tree to life.

I flick a text to Quinton asking just that.

When he replies that she would love to and is free Saturday, my face stretches with a smile that I feel all the way to my bones.

I can feel the weight lifting already.

The house is spotless. Me, however, not so much.

I strip the filthy clothes from my body and turn on the shower. Dad is in bed, out like a light again after a good dinner of roast beef, root vegetables, and steamed greens. I'm getting better at cooking up the basics, at least. His cocktail of meds for dessert had him sleepy in front of the television, which made moving him to his room difficult. But he'll sleep like the dead 'til early morning now.

Which is convenient, since I'm exhausted and in desperate need of a shower.

I can practically hear my bed and book calling my name.

Bare, I step into the steaming stream of water.

"Oh, that's so good."

I roll my head, letting the heated spray massage my neck and tight shoulders.

Pumping some shampoo into my hand, I lather it up before sliding it through my long, dark locks. It smells amazing, all apples and raspberries. It's always been my favorite.

It was Mom's. The one she used when we were kids.

If you associate memories with smell, then this scent is my mother, tangled in with every hug, every time she carried me when I was small or upset. The times she would lay in my bed to help me fall asleep or when I had a nightmare.

She's entrenched in my childhood. And in the person I'm becoming.

The pipework groans. I glance at the tile like I can see through it to the source of the noise.

When the tap whines and spurts out freezing water, I scream.

"Ah! Fuck. What the hell!"

I sidestep the icy water, grabbing for the tap, desperate to turn it off.

Instead, my footing slips in the shampoo suds, and my ass meets the now-freezing tile.

"FUCK."

Shivering, I clamber onto all fours. Every breath is staccato and burning as the deluge of water continues to freeze me to the bone, rendering me unable to move out of it fast enough.

Thundering footsteps close in down the hallway.

Glancing at the doorway, I haul my trembling limbs from the shower, one after the other. And when I come nose to toe with steel caps, my skin flushes with embarrassment.

At least I'm warmer.

"What the hell happened?" He squats, wrapping me in a towel.

I'm too cold to answer him, my teeth chattering to the point of chipping.

"Fuck, you're freezing."

Thank you, Captain Obvious. He hauls me to my feet, crushing me to his chest, his arms wrapping around my back as I stand dripping all over his boots. My hair is caked with suds.

"Your hot water crap out?" he says, eyeing the shower, still spluttering.

"S-some-fink, l-like dat." My teeth crash into each other.

With a groan, the water ebbs to a miserable dribble before stopping altogether.

"F-fuck," I mutter.

"I'll take a look at it in the morning. You want to try the downstairs bathroom?"

He releases me and takes a step back.

And I'm just standing here, his gaze traveling my body the only source of warmth I have. A girl should be grateful for that, I guess.

"S-sure."

"To save wandering around in the cold, I'll go and check if it's functional. If not, my place."

Before I have a chance to object, he's out the door. Hurried, thundering steps fall down the stairs. Still freezing, I grab another towel from the rack and slide it over my shoulders and sink onto the bathmat, crossing my legs and leaning over to conserve warmth.

I have to rinse my hair out, or it will be impossible in the morning.

A beat later, my flannel-clad neighbor is leaning on my bathroom doorframe. "No-go downstairs, I'm afraid. Get dressed and bring something warm, you can use my bathroom."

When my eyebrows rise dangerously close to my hairline, he adds, "The guest bathroom downstairs, Celeste. Don't get too excited." The stupid grin on his face sees me screw my own face up at him.

If my mood was any less stable, I'd poke my tongue out at him.

He steps inside the bathroom and extends a hand to me.

I take it. It's so warm. So big. It folds around mine as I pull myself to my feet. "Just give me a minute."

"Your dad's okay?"

"Yeah, asleep. He should be out for hours."

"I'll wait downstairs."

"Sure, thanks."

He hesitates before stepping out of the bathroom. And

it's only after he's left the cold space that I realize he must have heard me scream and come running.

Oh wow, that was . . .

Sweet?

The last word I'd associate with Quinton MacKelvie— at least, as per my original assessment of the grump next door.

Five minutes later, I'm bundled up and have a toiletry bag of essentials, ready for a deliciously hot shower. I'm more than ready to thaw my bones after the last ten minutes. Closing the door and locking it just in case, I walk across the snowy ground from my porch to Quinton's.

His is lit up like the North Pole, waiting for Santa to come home from a late-night flight. Just in case Rudolph loses his way . . .

Inside, he shows me to the guest bathroom and pulls the door shut tight.

Turning on the water, I'm elated to find it's almost scorching. I spend an inordinate amount of time letting my bones melt in the sweltering heat. As if that will erase the frigid fright I got or the fact that Quinton saw me naked on the floor . . .

And despite the heat circulating around the small space, my face heats further. *How embarrassing.* Is this going to make things super awkward now?

I finish up and dress, taking my time to brush out my hair and fix it into a long plait. A small knock rattles the door.

"CC, is that you?" a small voice says.

"Maise? You still up?"

"Daddy said I could say goodnight."

"Oh, okay. I'll be out in a sec."

Bundling my things back into the bag, I open the door. Maisey is in her reindeer pajamas, her hair braided, big eyes looking up as she slams into me. Her arms wrap around my waist, her face smooshed into my stomach. "Night, CC."

Her muffled words vibrate through my belly.

"Righto, little miss. Bedtime." Quinton's low tone sees Maise peel away, a little pout on her face before she schools it back.

"One more thing," she says, beckoning me down to her level with a finger.

"What is it, sweetheart?" I bend down, and she closes in like we're about to exchange secrets.

"There's mistletoe under the kitchen door," she whispers, loud enough for us all to hear.

I glance to Quinton, whose face is straining to stay neutral.

"Okay, don't tell your dad. We'll make it a surprise."

"He totally didn't notice yet."

"Mum's the word."

Her eyes light up as she nods quickly, lips pursed.

I kind of feel bad putting ideas into her head. But it's not like it didn't almost happen. And sometimes you just need a little hope, right? But the second the thought passes, I realize that getting her hopes up is cruel. She's so young, she probably has dreams of her father finding someone that will become part of their life permanently.

There's nothing permanent about my existence.

Shit.

I should have kept my mouth shut.

Before I can take back what I said, Quinton is ushering her up the stairs and to bed.

God, I'm a horrible human being. Planting ideas and dreams in the heads of young children, only so they can be ripped away . . .

May as well be the grinch.

I consider ducking out without saying goodnight, but that would be worse.

So I wait at the front door, bag in hand, gaze on the floor as I reprimand myself for my reckless stupidity with a little girl's heart.

"Must be an interesting patch of floor." His words are soft, low.

He clears his throat.

"Huh? Yeah, about before, I'm sorry if I gave Maisey the wrong ide—"

"The only wrong *anything* with this scenario is the doorway you're standing by."

"Right, she's going to expect that now."

I am truly an idiot.

"She's not the only one," he says, a grin widening his lips.

And my gaze is stuck on them.

The silence turns to tension-filled white noise as I raise my eyes to meet his. "Qui—"

"It's okay, Celeste. I don't . . ." He rubs a hand behind his neck, his gaze searching the room. "Nightcap?"

Tugging my bottom lip through my teeth, I shift on my feet before nodding. "Sure."

I drop my bag by the door, and he leads me into the living room. The fireplace crackles away, two stockings resting on the rustic wooden mantle above it. The entire room is bordered by garland and trimmed with strings of fairy lights.

Maisey sure went all out on this space.

"She loves Christmas so much, doesn't she?" I wander to the mantle, running my fingertips over the soft fabric of the stocking with Maisey's name on it. How long has it been since our family exchanged gifts? I can't remember. But a long time, that's for sure.

"She does. Easter and Fourth of July, too. My girl is big on events and the people she shares them with."

I glance back as he pours two fingers of something amber into two glasses. "That's incredible, Quinton."

Handing me a glass, he comes to stand by my side in front of the fire with a chuckle. "Tell that to my wallet."

"Oh, I bet." I take a sip. A slight burn continues all the way down, warming me from the inside.

"You still need help with your tree?"

"Um, yes. I could use Maisey's talent. Our house

looks . . ." I gaze at the flickering flames. "We haven't done Christmas for years." The last phrase is almost a whisper.

"You have the power to change that, you know."

I know.

"I guess."

"Cel—"

"I should get home."

I hand him the empty glass with a soft "thank you." He simply nods, rooted to the spot, a glass in each hand as I head for the front door.

When I reach the door, I hesitate, plucking my bag from the floor where I left it.

"Stop." The word is gravel and a little harsh.

I still like a deer in headlights, softening as he closes in. His sandalwood and spice hems me in by the door. My back hits it as my gaze is once again trained to his lips. He studies my face, a hand sliding across my cheek and into my hair. "Fuck, CC."

I huff out a strained breath.

My chest plummets with a fiery inhale with the electricity that sparks and travels through me with his touch.

"I really want to kiss you," he rasps.

His Adam's apple bobs as he waits for a response.

"We can't . . ."

FOURTEEN

QUINTON

My gut plummets. The one thing I've wanted. The only woman I've wanted for years . . . and she doesn't want to.

We can't.

"I—"

Her finger presses over my lips.

And fuck, her touch is so damn soft, it's torture. Her fragrant floral-and-cinnamon scent shrouds me. Her deep brown eyes take their time traveling my face as if taking stock.

"We can't kiss here. Mistletoe, remember?"

Relief and desire tangle into a heady concoction.

Her bag drops to the floor as her finger slips from my lips. I slide my arms around her waist, hauling her onto my hips. With a giggle, her hands find my face, and she whispers, "Hi."

"Hi, CC."

"Quin—"

I stride for the kitchen doorway. And when we find six clusters of mistletoe my daughter apparently managed to hang all by herself, both of us burst out laughing.

"Oh my god, she really, really wants you to kiss someone." CC's eyes are lit with amusement.

But the amusement fades when she notices my stone look. "Not someone, Celeste. You."

"Oh," she mutters, glancing up at the mistletoe assault hanging overhead. "Well, we wouldn't want to disappoint her."

"No," I rasp.

I lower her to her feet, and she looks up at me. It's then I see the desire darkening her gaze. The way her chest rises and falls too quickly.

"Put your arms around me," I say.

"Like this?" Her arms slide around my neck.

"Just like that. Now move closer."

"We're not close enough?" Cheekiness lines her tone.

"Not nearly."

"You are so bossy."

"You have no idea."

She scoffs an amused, slightly nervous sound. I can only imagine what she would feel like . . .

Heat flushes her face and neck as she drops her forehead to my chest. I could get used to this. Having her this close.

Having her, period.

When she peels off my chest and her gaze swings up to mine, I can't wait a second longer.

Palming her face, I drop my mouth to hers.

"Qui—"

I brush my lips over her silky, plump ones, barely tamping down the groan that wants out when her hands crawl into my hair. I coax her to open for me.

And she does.

I claim every part of her she gives up.

Head buzzing with an intensity I've never felt before, I break away, each short, useless breath burning its way through my chest as I study her face.

It's wrecked.

As wrecked as I feel.

I stand, struggling to regain my breath, as she starts shaking her head.

"Cel—"

"Oh my god . . ." She takes a step back. "I-I'm sorry."

She spins and rushes to the door. Plucking up her bag, she's across the threshold in a beat. The door hits the wall and remains open as she takes the porch steps two at a time, flying across the snowy ground to her house.

Fuck.

I pad to the front door and close it before letting my forehead hit the wood. Dammit.

"Daddy?"

I spin around to find Maise rubbing her eyes at the bottom of the stairs.

"Did CC go home?"

"Yeah, kiddo, she did. You okay?"

She yawns. She looks exhausted. I close the distance, haul her onto my waist, and trudge up the stairs. Rubbing a hand over her hair, I hold her close.

"Did my Christmas wish come true?" she says as I walk into her room.

"What wish was that?" I put her back in her bed and tuck her in tight, snug as a bug in a rug style.

"Under the mistletoe, Daddy."

I sit on the edge of the bed.

How do I answer that? She did, but I'm guessing the last part was not what she had envisioned. Besides, my heart is not her responsibility.

"A gentleman never kisses and tells, so I guess you'll never know, little lady. Now go back to sleep."

I tap her little nose, and she scrunches her face up. *Sassy little woman.*

"I guess I'll have to move to plan B, then," she says with a smile and rolls over, giving me her back.

Should I be scared?

"Night, Maise."

I rise and walk through the bedroom door, closing it most of the way.

"Night, Daddy. Don't dream about CC too much. Okay?"

Oh, I'm scared, alright. This little girl has got plans, and she'll be hell-bent on seeing them through. What's a guy to do?

Who am I to get in her way?

I chuckle as I make my way back downstairs.

In the kitchen, I wash up the glasses and glance out the window to light snow coming down. It coats every surface with its pale glittering powder. It's pretty, sparkling under the streetlights, the Christmas lights from our house, and the crescent moon overhead.

Movement catches my attention from next door. CC is in her kitchen, pajamas on now, pulling a bottle of water from the fridge before she pads from the room, flipping the light switch and leaving the space in darkness. Leaving me staring at the dim house as I work through what the hell that kiss was.

I could devour that woman and still starve for her.

But it's not just my heart in this.

There's four of us, if you count Maise and Hank.

I've already seen Maise live through the realization her mother didn't want her. I couldn't do that to her again.

It would be beyond cruel.

And that's the sole reason I've never come this far with anyone before.

It's not just my heart that will be shattered all over the damn floor if things don't work out.

I wipe the counter down and double-check the fridge and pantry, noting the items I need from the store tomorrow before heading upstairs.

After showering, I settle into bed, running through the tasks remaining to have the school play assets completed and functional.

But that just brings me back to Celeste.

Hell, I couldn't fight this even if I wanted to.

"**Y**ou're doing it wrong." Celeste's gaze burns into mine.

"I'm not. This is what the plans have marked out."

"Well, I'm pretty sure they want the wheels to actually roll the backdrop frame in and out, which means sideways." She gestures with her hands. "Onstage"—she swings an arm to the right then to the left—"offstage."

I tilt my head, closing my eyes. I can't think straight with CC this close. When was the last time I made a mistake at work?

Like, never.

I'm calling it collateral damage from that kiss last night. And I'm assuming the attitude I'm currently getting from her is a coping mechanism. Because there is no way she wasn't just as affected as I was.

With a sigh, I say, "Guess that makes sense."

"Thank you!" She throws her arms up in exasperation.

I see she's a good sport about me losing.

And what I wouldn't give to kiss that smug look off her beautiful face.

Instead, since Maise and Hank are watching us like we're the main characters in some blockbuster movie, I tousle her hair with my hand playfully and say, "You're welcome."

"Whatever, MacKelvie."

I wince. "MacKelvie, ouch."

She gives me a sarcastic face before wandering over to her backdrops. They're almost done—only the finer details left to go, which she is painting today. She's amazing to watch. It's like she just knows where everything goes, what shades and colors need to make up each stroke of her brush.

I decide it's better to just get on with our tasks, what with it being Saturday, before either of my two helpers lose interest.

"Right, you two. The lady has spoken, wheels operating side to side. Maise, you're in charge of the two on the right of the frame. Hank, you and I will get the lefts knocked up."

His eyes round to saucers.

Oh geez, wrong choice of words. Sure, my head has been in the gutter and in the clouds all at once since I kissed his daughter, who is now mere feet from where we stand. Fighting the flush of heat threatening to engulf my face, I clear my throat. I can salvage this, I think.

"How about we screw the—"

Hank's face splits with laughter. Maise frowns in confusion. And me? I stand there dumbfounded, only just real-izing he's been messing with me this entire time.

"Someone has a thing for the pretty little artist who's been helping us," Hank whispers as he leans in like it's a huge conspiracy.

That pretty little artist is your damn daughter, bud. It would be funny otherwise. It would be appropriate, maybe, if I didn't feel like I was stealing candy canes from an old man—straight out of his Alzheimer-ridden hands.

"Nah, just didn't get much sleep last night." I run a hand through my hair.

Hank's face says it all. I'm not fooling anyone.

Much less myself.

Maybe it's a good thing Hank's got no clue. If he did . . .

It's unknown territory for me, this disease of his. And I'm glad Celeste has a little fire in her, or this new phase of her life would be much harder.

Maise sinks to the floor by the feet of the frame, her screwdriver with a pink glittery handle in her hand. She's been helping me for a while now and insisted on her own tools.

I watch as she sticks her tongue out one side of her mouth, screwing the metal plate of the wheel into the pine two-by-four. One little hand works the tool, the other holding the hardware in place as she sinks all four screws into place before tightening them in turn.

Hank groans, his hand slipping as he kneels over the frame, the caster wheel in his other hand.

Shit.

I drop down beside him and hold the wheel in place as he secures it to the frame. When all four are attached, we manhandle the frame back onto its feet and stand back.

"Looking great, boss." Hank slaps my back.

I chuckle.

He's good company, despite his memory being shot. And I imagine when he was fully cognitive, he was a hell of a guy.

"That looks wonderful," a light voice says.

I turn back to find CC, her face streaked with blue paint, paintbrush still in hand. A wisp of hair has slipped from her ponytail, sticking to her cheek with the same blue hue.

"Thanks. How's the scenery coming along?"

"All done. Just a little cleanup left now."

"You could say that." I can't help the grin that blooms as her face falls and tightens with a self-conscious look. I lean in and brush the strand of hair from her face. "Blue looks good on you."

"Huh." She dips her head, a blush coloring her cheeks.

"Daddy, can we go? I'm starving." Maise brings me back to reality, hands on hips, gaze swinging between me and Celeste.

"Sure, kiddo. Pack up your tools."

She skips back to her workspace and packs her things in her pink tool belt. When she was a baby, she would come on-site with me, pink hard hat and all. Wasn't a contractor on-site not affected by her cute little mug. The hard hat still sits in her cupboard, but now she's upgraded to the tool belt, and I couldn't be more proud of her.

"Actually, Maise," Celeste says, getting her attention. "Would you be free tonight to help me with the tree?"

Celeste presses her hands together in a pleading gesture, using my daughter's favorite tool of manipulation against her. *Touché.*

Maise shoulders her tool belt and comes to my side. "Sure, CC. I can help you out. How's seven sound?"

I chuckle as Celeste's eyebrows raise toward her hairline before she flattens her smile and simply says, "Sounds perfect, see you then."

"Yep, it's a date." Maise winks at her.

Oh no, what is she up to . . . ?

CHAPTER

FIFTEEN

CELESTE

Pacing by the tree, I check the clock for the third time in five minutes. With my hot water fixed—thanks to Quinton's endless source of contacts—I'm showered, fed, and waiting on my Christmas stylist like I'm on hold for a damn lung transplant.

My gut flips, sending wild butterflies throughout my stomach.

Shit.

I wring my hands as I turn back and stalk around the room, righting the few trinkets and pieces of decor this old house has had since, well, forever. I fluff up the aged curtains, tying them back with the decorative white ropes that hang from small gold hooks by the window frame.

I tug at the fabric when it refuses to budge along the curtain rod.

Dust and crumbling drywall fall from above. With a

groan, the rod plummets to the floor. I jump back, barely missing a curtain rod-induced concussion.

"Oh shit!"

So much for my Christmas decorating attempts.

The front door rattles under a heavy knock.

Great, just great. The living room is a mess . . .

Shaking my head, I walk to the door and open it to find Maisey standing in front of her father, who is currently straining to hold up a giant box. Said box has tinsel spewing from it. A split down one corner reveals glittering baubles.

"What is all this?" I say, opening the door and stepping aside.

Quinton walks into the living room. He stops short when he spies the tree and the fallen curtain rod, loosing a low chuckle. "Damn, CC. You really do need our help."

"Step aside, Daddy." Maise looks up at him so seriously. "I got this."

He drops the box in the center of the room and salutes his daughter before coming to stand beside me. "You sure you know what you signed up for?"

"Yes? No . . ."

"Hank watching the game?"

"Yep. In the TV room."

He pats me on the shoulder like some long-lost bud. "Godspeed, baby."

His face is all empathy that twists to amusement as he wanders down the hallway.

Ass.

And . . . now that's the only place my gaze wants to be. His perfect, jean-clad ass saunters away from me like he knows I'm watching. The balls on this guy. I chuckle and he glances over his shoulder. This time, it's him who hesitates by the door.

His focus is trained on me as his throat bobs.

Dammit.

For a heartbeat I forget he's a single dad, the annoying guy next door, and a constant reminder of how incapable I am as a grown-ass adult. And I just . . . *see* him.

My chest plummets as the need to be anywhere but out of his orbit overwhelms m—

Shit, no.

Not happening, Celeste.

We are not falling for the flannel-clad contractor next door. No matter how stupidly handsome, kind, and considerate he is.

Not doing it.

My life is complicated enough.

"This all has to go." Maisey's words snap me from the trance I'm in.

Quinton's head tilts back just a little as he slaps a hand to the doorframe and disappears into the TV room.

I turn back to find Maisey ripping the few strings of tinsel and handful of ancient decorations from the tree.

"Those are the only things I had."

"I know. That's why I got Daddy to bring you some more. This tree is just sad."

I chuckle and nod. She is totally right.

"You know what? We need some music, sweetheart."

"Ooh yes! Something fun."

Maisey's head disappears into the oversized box as I slide my phone from my pocket and tap the screen to find Christmas music.

When I scroll through all the tunes, I come across "Rockin' Around the Christmas Tree". Perfect.

Turning the volume up, I race to the kitchen and find the biggest metal mixing bowl I can, setting my phone in it to amplify the sound. I rest it on the sofa, and we get to work. Dancing as we decorate, I follow the very detailed instructions from my holiday stylist until not only the tree is a spectacle in itself, but the room is absolutely spectacular, too.

"Last thing," Maisey says, holding out a large light-up star to me. "You may do the honors."

"Thanks, Maise."

She beams at me. And I place the star on the very top.

"Wait!" Maisey says, hitting the light switch for the living room lights. "Daddy!"

Quick, heavy steps close in a heartbeat later, and she turns back to me with a double thumbs up.

I flick the small toggle on the star's battery box, and the entire room lights up under its golden glow.

But when I turn back, the only person left in the living room with me is Quinton.

Ah, she totally set us up . . .

Little trickster.

"Well played, kiddo," Quinton murmurs, the quiet words sending something visceral through me, his eyes burning into mine.

"Ta-da," I say with strained enthusiasm, holding my arms out toward the impressive tree. "Isn't she beautiful?"

But Quinton's eyes don't stray from my face to the tree, not for a second as he closes the distance between us. "Beautiful, stunning, thoughtful . . . selfless."

He's so close, every sense I own is infiltrated by him.

"We still talking about the tree?" I whisper.

He shakes his head as his palms collect my jaw, tilting my face up to his. "Nope."

He caresses my face, his thumbs trailing over my cheekbones and brushing over my mouth before snagging on my bottom lip. "I haven't stopped thinking about the last time you let me kiss you, Celeste."

I'm barely huffing out viable breaths, let alone forming words, and my eyes flutter shut. "Is this a good idea? What about Maise?"

"Honestly, I have no idea. But I can't see this turning out any other way."

"And what way is that?" I narrow my eyes playfully, curling my fingers around his hands still holding my face.

"I would rather show you than the—"

"Oh, kiss her already, Daddy!"

I huff a surprised sound as Quinton groans, his forehead pressing to mine.

"You heard the little lady," he rasps.

"I did." I press up on my toes and drag his mouth down to mine.

His hands tilt my head a little further and he claims my mouth the way he did the first time. Not making him wait this time, I open and he's everywhere. Hands, tongue, lips . . .

My skin is electrified where his hands grip my face. Each choppy breath sends my head higher and higher as my center melts, and I can't get close enough.

His body presses against mine. Heat pools low in my belly. My hands grip his hair like a lifeline, and I . . . can't breathe . . .

Breaking away, I rasp, "Quin—"

He holds me steady, his grip firm around my biceps as I try like hell to ground myself. Unlike last time, I have no intention of running away. For the first time in my life, I am desperate for something to stick. If not forever, for as long as it is good.

"Must be some tree." My father's voice has us turn toward him in unison. Maisey stands by him, and they high five like they planned this all along. But I know that's impossible. With a spotty memory, Dad's not likely to be able to do anything of the sort. But his single moment of clarity around what's happening here? I'll take it.

"How was the game, Hank?" I ask.

"Ah, rubbish. We lost, again." He waves a hand and wanders down the hall.

Well, there you go. Two moments of clarity. Maise is in our space the second Dad's gone. "So now can you kiss and tell?" She looks up at Quinton.

He simply chuckles, sweeping her up into his arms. "Hmm, looks like it's your bedtime."

"Oh no, I was helping," she whines.

"Yes, you were. But every girl needs their beauty sleep."

"Even CC?"

Quinton adjusts her on his hip. "Even CC."

She slaps his arm. "Daddy, don't say that. She'll think you don't like her."

The look of utter horror on her face almost has me doubled over. But I restrain myself and add, "I would love to go to bed early, Maise. We can build snowmen tomorrow if we get enough sleep, just us girls."

"Really?!"

"Sure thing."

"Yes!" She pumps a fist into the air. "Hear that, Daddy? You're not invited."

He narrows his eyes at her playfully. "If you say so, kiddo."

Snow drifts from the sky as if it's totally on board with our snowman building plans. Of course it is.

Maise sits at the kitchen counter as I pour out hot cocoa to warm ourselves with before we brave the frosty outdoors. The front door slams, and I assume it's Quinton.

Heavy footfalls tell me my assumption was spot-on. He rounds the doorway and crosses the checkered tile to drop onto a stool by his daughter.

"You forgot your beanie, Maise."

Tugging it over her head, he gives me the brightest smile as the beanie covers her eyes.

She's batting his hands away a second later, and I return the smile before Maisey's eyes emerge from the woolen shroud.

"Morning, Celeste," Quinton rasps.

I pull out an extra cup and slide two full mugs over the counter before pouring my own. The cupboard overhead has marshmallows and powdered sugar, so I grab them, and we douse our drinks in the sugary nonsense.

"Thought I heard someone come in," Dad says, sliding onto a stool on the other side of Maisey.

Gang's all here.

Maisey turns to my father. "We're building a snowman. Did you want to help?"

"Sounds like fun, little miss. Count me in." His hands come to rest on the counter with a slight tremble. An early warning sign of a not-so-great day. Maybe some sunshine will help.

"You know what, I think that's a great idea." I pass Dad a mug of hot cocoa.

"Thanks, love." He takes a sip, wincing when the liquid burns.

Shit.

"Careful, Hank. It might need more milk."

He slides it back over and I add a little extra to cool it down.

Maisey looks sheepish. "But I guess it's not just us girls, then."

"One more couldn't hurt, could it?" I ask her.

"Suppose not." She swirls a finger in her drink, bumping the marshmallows against the side of the mug.

Dad slides his mug back to me, shaking his head. "Come on, young lass. Let's get started."

He stands and brushes down his clothes. I take a beat to check he's warm enough before adding, "Don't forget your coats."

Dad simply nods, and Maisey takes his hand as they walk into the hall. Maisey doesn't give him a second before she's quizzing his snowman-making skills in great detail.

"You think he'll have a good day?" Quinton asks.

"Not sure. He has a bit of a tremor. Hopefully some fresh air will help."

It takes me a moment to realize what he's really asking— is Maisey safe with my father today? And it's a valid question with a valid reason behind it.

"They should be okay for a few minutes. Did you have something in mind?"

He's off the stool and crowding me against the counter in the space of a heartbeat. In a tangle of sandalwood and spice, his hands wrap around my neck and weave into my hair.

"You could say that," he whispers, his lips brushing the shell of my ear.

My brain is short-circuiting, and I know I have something to tide us over for a little while, but I can't think straight with his hands on me. I—

"Camera . . . app . . ." I squeak as he nips my neck.

"Mhmmm, very useful. You want to record this?"

"What? No!"

He chuckles and puts a little space between us.

"On my phone. The security app has the front and back of the house on it. So if I need to duck out, I can keep an eye on Dad. Since he has a history of running away."

"So what you're saying is that we can fool around for a little while and they will be okay outside?" One brow arches, the intensity of his gaze sending hot flushes through my body.

"Well, I'm not saying we can't . . ."

"How very cryptic, *Celeste*."

"*Quinton*."

"You know, you don't have to use every syllable in my name every damn time."

I tilt my head. He wants me to—

"Just Quin is fine, baby."

"Oh," I breathe as he eliminates the space between us.

"That okay with you?"

"Uh-huh."

It's all I can do to nod when his hands cup my face, and he claims my mouth. When he wants in, I open, melting against the marble countertop.

I'm on fire, and nowhere near close enough.

My clothes feel like sandpaper on my skin. Heat pools low in my belly, as his hand moves down my neck. My own are planted on his heaving chest. Every breath he takes rubs my now-hard peaks in the most torturous way. But he breaks away.

"No, please don't stop," I gasp.

"Fuck, I don't ever want to do that . . . But you have far too many layers on."

"It's cold."

He chuckles, leaning in close again. "I can think of a few ways to warm you up."

Oh god.

I nip his jaw. "Then what are you waiting for?"

A warm hand slips under my sweater and shirt, caressing my belly with his knuckles. "Fuck, you are so soft. I can only imagine how incredible the rest of you is."

"Only one way to find out, Quin."

We both glance at my phone, checking the video footage. Maise and Dad are rounding up haphazard piles of snow. And they don't have anywhere enough for one snow-man, let alone two. We have heaps of time.

"Plenty of time," Quin rasps. "How do want me to use it, CC?"

"Wisely?" I ask, screwing my face up.

He grumbles something before sliding his hands further up my belly. When his fingers meet my bra, they skirt the hard underwire before slipping underneath.

His touch is ethereal.

Sparks scatter along my skin over every inch his finger-tips travel. And I'm dying to kiss him. Taste him. Close the space between us even further. "Quin, please."

"This kitchen door lock?" His voice is low and gravelly.

I nod. "Marie used to lock us out when she was cooking Sunday roasts years ago."

He strides to the door and closes it, locking it tight.

Fingers digging into her waist, I lift her onto the counter. A little breath huffs past her parted lips when her ass meets the hard countertop. I position myself between her legs, and she leans in, tilting my head up as she claims my mouth. I love this side of CC—the side that knows what she wants and fucking takes it.

Because I plan on doing the same thing.

Lifting her sweater and shirt out of my way, I claim a hard peak through her lacy red bra. Her thighs fall apart even more, her hands gravitating to my hair as she whimpers. What I wouldn't give to have nothing between us.

But this isn't about me.

I've had years to figure that out.

When it comes to women: for best results, apply selflessness. Hell, I learned most of it from my daughter.

Soft flesh gives way under my grip as I tug a hip toward me. "Dammit, CC. How is it possible that I can't get you close enough?"

She stills, big blown-out brown eyes staring down at me. Her hand runs over my jawline as her mouth parts on a ragged breath.

She's fucking stunning.

Her pretty red lips swollen from my kiss.

Her face flushed from my touch.

And it's not enough. Glancing at the video feed on her phone only to see the start of one odd-looking snowman, I decide we've wasted enough time.

I release the clasp of her bra, and her hands sink into my hair, their grip renewed around my tousled locks. Neither of us is slowing down. Hell, I'm not certain I'll ever recuperate from seeing Celeste undone this way, and we've barely started.

"Quin," she mutters. "I—"

I take a long, languid suckle of her peak, and she bucks off the counter. My grip tightens around her hips as I do it again.

The softest, most intoxicating mewl slips past her lips.

"Fuck, CC."

"God, we should really be building a snowman," she whines.

I chuckle at her assessment of our current situation. But as the amusement fades, burned out by the overwhelming desire for her that has me rock-fucking-hard right now, I shift to the other peak. Grabby hands tug at my flannel shirt, then at the T-shirt beneath it, until her fingertips trace the lines of my stomach and upward over my chest. "I want to see you."

I release the nipple with a pop and tug the shirt from my back.

CC sits on the edge of the counter, breathless.

When she swallows, somewhat regaining her composure, she says, "How am I supposed to live next door to this?" An elegant hand waves at my exposed torso. "You're going to have to sleep naked and leave your curtain open, Quinnie."

I raise a brow. "That was fast."

She huffs a nervous sound. "What was?"

"The nickname."

"I can nix it if you hate it."

I step closer, my body pressing against hers as I cup the back of her neck with my hand. "There's not one thing about you I could ever hate, CC."

Her face flattens under something that looks suspiciously like shock. "I mean—"

"Daddy! CC! Come see our snowman!" Maisey's voice carries through the phone app, the faded echo of it outside reaching us through the closed door.

"Shit, that's our cue," CC says, pulling her sweater down.

"Let me fix you up," I offer.

She turns to give me her back, and I do the clasp of the bra up. Not able to resist, I wrap myself around her one last time. "To be continued, neighbor."

Her hand reaches back, running through my hair as she turns her face and dots a kiss to my jawline. "I'll hold you to that, Quin."

I'm damn sure of it.

We unlock the door and head for the backyard. Pushing out into the morning sun, we find Maise helping Hank sink sticks into the side of the snowman for arms.

All . . . seven of them?

Interesting . . .

"Hey kiddo, your man here has a few too many arms." I point at the multi-armed creation, realizing now he is more alien than snowman.

"Hank wanted to do something different. He kept saying 'we need more, Tisha, more.'"

"I see." I come to stand behind Maise, wrapping my arms around her as I dot a kiss to the top of her beanie. The cold day's wind whips at my back, reminding me that, in our rush, we forgot our coats.

"Daddy," Maisey says, looking up at me. "Who's Tisha?"

"CC's mama," I whisper into her ear, not wanting to confuse Hank.

CC gives me a grateful look as she adjusts Hank's coat and scarf.

"Are you and CC going to build a snowman, too?" Maisey says, bending down and scooping up a handful of snow, holding it out to me.

"Maybe. CC, you up for building a snowman with me?"

"Sure, just let me get Hank inside. Then you're on, MacKelvie."

"Sounds like a challenge, not a team effort."

She leads her father to the back of the house, settling him in his reading chair where she can keep an eye on him, and returns, her smile blazing through the crisp winter surroundings.

"What do you think, Maise? Us girls against your dad?"

"Yes!" Maise leaves me in the dust—well, snow— quicker than a cat up a tree with its tail on fire, sticking her tongue out at me for good measure.

"Right, you're on. First to build a regular snowman wins."

"Hold up, let's set some parameters first." CC cocks a hip, planting a hand to it.

"What's a pawameter?" Maise scrunches up her face.

"The things that each snowman has to have." CC wriggles her brows at her. "Like two arms, three buttons on his chest, two eyes, a nose, and a mouth. Okay, Quinnie?"

The cheeky damn smile stretching her face is going to keep me up later. But sure, I can agree to that. "Deal. We start in three . . . two . . . one . . . Go!"

The girls rush about gathering snow as Maise giggles. Celeste cackles at her when they slip into each other and snow flies everywhere. I squat, raking snow into a pile until I have enough for the first round section. The girls are doing more laughing than building. But I guess that's the point to all this.

Thirty minutes later, and between three out-of-breath, snow-covered people, we have two-ish snowmen. Mine is super basic. The girls went all out, giving theirs accessories and stick hair.

They're damn hilarious.

CC comes to stand by my side as the self-appointed snowman judge, a.k.a. Maisey, walks with her hands behind her back, eyeing each one in turn.

"Hmmm. Ten points for a structurally sound snowman, Daddy. But that's all. You have no flair."

CC's shoulders shake as she slaps a hand over her mouth.

"CC, our—I mean, *your* snowman . . . has all the trimmings. I declare you the clear winner!" She rushes CC, who is now shaking from the cold and not from laughing at my John Doe snowman. CC bends down, hugging her tight.

"Group hug, Daddy!"

I fold myself around them both without hesitation. And the look of pure joy I get from Maisey all but seals the deal on my back-and-forth about including Celeste in our lives.

How could a guy say no to that face?

"As warm as your hugs are, I'm absolutely freezing, Maise. Can we go inside now?" CC begs.

Maisey hugs her tighter but relents. "Sure. We need to celebrate in style, anyways . . ."

Maise leads CC inside by the hand, and I follow behind, watching as they chatter away about future projects, snowmen, and this Christmas season.

It almost feels like a new normal.

Almost.

An elementary-aged boy dressed up as an elf gives us a bored look as I hand over our two tickets to the school's Christmas play at the gymnasium doors. Maisey bounces around me as we make our way inside. The gymnasium has been transformed into a winter wonderland, mirroring outside but more . . . magical?

I flick a text to CC. Knowing her, she has Hank squared away somewhere inside already.

"Oh, Daddy, look! Can we sit with Hayley from my class?"

A small blonde girl is standing on a chair further up, waving at us.

"Sure, let's grab a seat before people start filing in."

We shuffle sideways in the third row until Maise is in the chair by Hayley's mom. At least, I think that's who it is.

The small blonde girl jumps up and whispers into Maisey's ear. And Maise is shaking her head.

"But we organized this," Hayley says, her brows dropping.

"That was before," Maise says softly.

"Before what?" Hayley throws her hands up.

"CC."

Now she has my attention. I check my phone for a reply as I listen to the two girls.

Nada.

That's odd.

The two girls whisper about whatever it is before Hayley pouts, her arms folded over her chest as she stalks back to her seat.

I lean down to Maise. "What's that all about?"

"Nothing." She fidgets on her seat. The new dress she insisted on for the big event looks about as comfortable as a straitjacket. She tugs at the turtleneck and flops back.

"Guess I'm down to no friends again," she mutters.

"Hey, wha—"

"Good evening, everyone!" The lights dim as the microphone squeals, now clutched in the principal's hand. "And welcome to our annual Christmas play. The children have been so excited for this. So, without further delay, I give you *A Starry Christmas Night*."

She waves an arm to one side as she leaves the small, low stage that takes up the entire short end of the gymnasium. CC is going to miss it.

Dammit.

All her hard work, and she's not here to see it.

The stage lights burst to life, illuminating the backdrop a beat later. It's incredible. Gasps come from the crowd alongside whispers about who the artist was for the over-sized painting. And more and more discussion arises about CC's work as the lights fixate on the empty stage too long.

When—finally—a disembodied arm pushes a small child past the side curtain, people quiet down, shifting in their seats.

A small boy, around six, all but cowers in the center of the stage. When it looks like he's about to cry, an older girl dressed as a fairy comes out and holds his hand. She nods, smiling down at him.

He pulls a small slip of paper from his elf pants and speaks.

"One night . . . long ago in the realm of the Christmas Fairy, something strange was a-afoot . . ."

Maisey sits up, hands clasped in her lap, gaze set on the stage like a kid getting her first glance at a candy store.

I check my phone again. My message still says unread.

Worry twists low in my gut.

But I flick Caleb a text. Maybe he can get her to answer. My ego isn't bigger than my concern for CC's safety. I force myself to stay in the damn seat and let my daughter enjoy her first Grafton Christmas play.

The second the engine splutters out, I'm out the door and bundling Maise inside our house. "Stay here, okay?"

She's not listening. The red and blue flashing lights in front of CC's house have her little face stricken. Caleb texted back halfway through the play, said there was an incident at Hank's house but that he had it handled. Now, seeing the ambulance and the paramedics at their house, I wish like hell we'd come home.

"Daddy, is CC okay?" Maise's face is distraught.

"I'm sure the car is there for Hank. You go change into your pajamas and put the television on, okay? I'll be back in a few minutes."

I grip her little face in my hands and plant a kiss to her forehead. The look of worry lining her eyes is so damn intense.

Did I make the wrong call not leaving the concert?

Sensing the urgency of the situation, she hurries inside, already pulling the long turtleneck dress off as soon as her coat is off her shoulders.

"Door, Maise."

She kicks it shut, and I stride for CC's house. I barely make it onto the porch before a gloved hand shoots out, stopping me in my tracks.

"Sir, I'm going to have to ask you to wait outside," a paramedic says. The tone of their voice is all wrong. Too apologetic.

"Nope, not happening." I push past and cross the front door threshold. The pressure in my chest has blood thundering in my ears.

"Sir! We are still fixing her up."

Her . . .

SEVENTEEN

CELESTE

Caleb moves from the doorway just as the paramedic in front of me dabs the nasty cut on my cheek. I hiss at the pain, and she apologizes for the umpteenth time since they started cleaning up my face.

I don't know what happened.

One minute we were getting ready to go out for the school play, the next, Dad was in a rage, shaking old photos in my face. I've seen him get upset and confused before, maybe even a little rough with the household things. But never has he laid a finger on me.

And the sad part is, he doesn't realize he's doing it, or who he's doing it to.

The man I grew up with never would hav—

"Fucking hell, CC," a low tone growls.

Quin.

Warm arms swallow me up as the paramedic is jostled out of the way. A heavy groan filters past my ear as sandalwood and spice shroud me.

Quin.

Relief crashes over me like a tidal wave.

And it only takes my body a second to register safety. Sagging against him, the first semblance of a sob slips through. Quin tightens around me, and I breathe him in. The total and overwhelming feeling of exhaustion consumes me.

It's been three weeks, but they have felt like years. Constantly worrying, busy with every task to make my father's days more comfortable and less confusing.

And still, it wasn't enough.

It's not enough.

A large, warm hand rubs over my back, reminding me I'm only wearing a shirt and no sweater. Trembling against him, I raise my head, just a little.

Caleb hovers outside the kitchen doorway, his cap in his hand. If he hadn't shown up when he did . . .

No. I refuse to believe my father would knowingly hurt me. That's not who he is.

Was, I guess.

This disease has warped his mind in so many ways.

Pushing the depressing thoughts from my head, I put space between us.

Quinton's eyes narrow as his jaw feathers. "Are you alright?"

"I'm okay."

His thumb traces the angle of my cheekbone, just under the nasty cut I received from a flying soup bowl I'd left on the draining rack by the sink. Quin steps out of the room, talking to Caleb. I listen to them speak in low tones. "What happened?"

"I got here, and Hank was yelling and tossing stuff. CC was trying to protect herself in the kitchen. But he tossed that bowl, and . . ."

"Fucking hell. I should've been here."

"Nobody saw this coming, bud. Least of all CC."

Quin sighs heavily. "Still. That's the last time I send another man to do my own damn job."

A strained chuckle spills from Caleb. "I bet."

Remembering I haven't cleaned the mess up, I pace in a fluster, opening cupboards and trying to locate the dustpan and broom.

The paramedic tries to intercept, and I ignore her.

"Someone out there loves you," she says softly. Her face is all mushy from the sentiment.

"It's not like that." I try another cupboard.

"Oh, kind of sounds like it." She gives me a conspiratorial smile.

Lord . . . small towns.

When I've opened every cupboard thrice, I'm blocked by an imposing wall of muscle. "CC," he says softly, hands closing around my arms. "I'll clean it up. Let the medic finish. Caleb's here if I need a hand, okay?"

It's all I can do to nod as he guides me by the shoulders to the counter stool.

"Almost done, hon," the paramedic says before dabbing the cut with something that burns and applying a dressing. "That should keep you out of trouble." She smiles, so genuinely.

But I doubt me and trouble will ever part ways.

I have a knack for letting it hunt me down. I just never thought it would take the form of my own father.

Alzheimer's—one.

CC—zero.

"You need anything, Celeste?" Caleb asks, hat in hand.

"No. Sorry you had to come all the way across town," I murmur.

He glances to Quinton. "Boss's orders."

My gaze swings between the two. "I—"

"It was no trouble, I'm just glad you're alright. Mostly, that is." Caleb nods and retreats from the doorway. A minute later his truck fires up and the sound disappears down the street.

Quinton is on his hands and knees, sweeping the porcelain shards into the dustpan.

"Quin—"

"Nope, not yet, baby. I need a minute. Go check on your dad."

Running my bottom lip through my teeth, I turn on my heel, slowly, and head for the living room.

Two paramedics sit with him on the sofa. He was given

something to calm down after they arrived. Caleb boxed him in so he couldn't hurt me again.

And my heart aches for my dad.

He's shaking his head, his face twisted with emotion as he repeats, "I didn't mean to hurt her, I didn't."

He rocks back and forth on the seat, arms hugged around his body.

And in this moment, he looks so small.

Nothing like the father I once knew, full of life. Ever so capable and a fierce defender of his family.

Leaning on the door, I purse my lips together as a hot tear tracks down my face and drips from my jaw. This is hurting him as much as it is me.

This lousy, shitty disease.

The aggression that took hold of him tonight makes the memory loss feel like a walk in the park. That is easily navigated. This? This is layers of emotions that I don't have the first clue how to deal with.

Finally, one paramedic notices me in the doorway and waves me in.

I pad to the sofa and stop in front of Dad. "Hank?"

His face cracks on a breathy sob. "I'm so sorry, Celeste."

Clarity.

Fleeting, blissful, damn painful clarity.

"Yeah, Daddy, I know. It's okay."

"No, no it's not. I—" He grinds his jaw shut, hands wringing in his lap.

"We've offered Hank a bed tonight to give you a short respite, and he's agreed."

"But won't that, you know, confuse him even more?" I glance at my father who still looks like he's with us in mind if not in spirit.

"Maybe, but we are responsible for the wellbeing of you both. And our senior medic thinks it's a good call."

"No. I feel like I'm sending him away for making a mistake."

My father doesn't say anything, but I can see in his eyes that he is already turning in on himself.

"He'll be fine here. This is his home. We'll be fine."

"Are you absolutely sure?"

"I am."

She stands and hands me a card. "If you change your mind, any unit can come at any time for transport to respite."

She gives me the wide-eyed look people do when they want to make sure you're paying attention.

"Okay, thank you."

"Do you have someone who can stay with you two?" She glances behind me.

I look over my shoulder to find Quin leaning on the same frame I just was.

"I live next door. I can be here if she needs me." He steps into the room.

"Good." The paramedic's focus is back on me. "Make sure you take him up on his offer."

I simply nod, and the paramedics gather their bags and equipment before walking out the front door.

"I'll make you a cup of tea and get your medication, Hank."

He stares straight ahead, not responding.

Deciding to just get it ready anyway, I head for the door.

"One sugar, a little milk, please, miss." His voice has returned to its usual lilt.

A sad smile tugs at my mouth, and Quinton follows me to the kitchen.

"Does he need a snack with his pills?" Quin says, rummaging through the pantry. When he pulls out a small pack of Christmas cookies, he slides them across the counter to me. I put the kettle on to boil and grab a mug.

Best Dad in the World is wrapped around the outside, the handle a bright blue, a hammer and screwdriver painted at the end of the phrase. Tears burn behind my eyes, like I haven't shed enough of those tonight.

"Hey, come here." Quinton rounds the counter and has me in his hold before my tears have the chance to fall. "None of this is your fault. You do an incredible job looking after your father, CC. A task most would have palmed off to some respite or old folks' home by now."

His hand travels over the back of my hair, and the sorrow that was threatening my undoing gives way to something more intense. I press closer to him, but pain lances through my face when pressure reaches the cut. With a hiss,

I make space. Quinton's hands are quick to palm my jawline, tilting my head up.

"A little bruising has started to come out, but otherwise still as beautiful as ever, baby."

I huff a breath and my eyes flutter shut briefly, before pushing to my toes. "Not so bad yourself, Mr. MacKelvie." I mess up his hair, and he dips his head forward, making it fall into his eyes. Dark blues look out from behind hooded eyes and light brown messy strands of hair.

I want to positively eat him.

Nothing has ever been surer in this world.

The kettle whistles, bursting our little bubble of intimacy. I turn back to the hot water and pour Dad's tea. Quin rummages through the drawers until he produces a tray and slides the cookies and mug onto it before stealing it away. "I've got it, you get ready for bed."

"What about Maise?"

"Oh, she's going to be so excited to see you."

My brows drop. "What do you mean?"

"You are sleeping at my house tonight, no arguments. I'll keep an eye on Hank."

"Qui—"

"Uh-uh, not negotiable, baby."

I round the counter and follow him through the door into the hallway. When he turns right heading for the living room, I go left. He makes it almost to the arch that leads into the living room when I say, "If you say so, Quinnie."

I sway my hips, taking the steps slowly and one at a time.

His eyes burn into me as I ascend the stairs. And I half imagine him dropping the tray and ravishing me over the steps. At least that way, one good thing would have come out of tonight.

But he gives me the most incredible smile before stepping into the living room and out of sight.

And my body is on fire.

From that one look, that one handsome-as-hell smile.

It's going to be a long night.

Maise is, as predicted, beside herself with excitement. She's jumping on her bed like a literal monkey, her chocolate curls flying around her shoulders as she squeals with delight.

"This is the best day ever!"

I chuckle. "I'm glad you're happy, sweetheart."

She slows, moving to the edge where I stand as she cuddles me tight. "Thank you for coming to my house," she whispers.

"Any time, snuggle bug."

She giggles again. But the tinkly sound peters out when her small hand touches my jaw. "Does it hurt where you fell and hit your head?"

"A little, but I feel much better here with you."

"Yeah, I'm pretty good company," she says with an exaggerated sigh that could win a stinking Oscar.

When she settles down and we slide into her bed, she snuggles up so close I'm afraid I'll roll over and smother her in her sleep.

"You comfy, snuggle bug?"

"Uh-huh, are you?"

"Yeah, I'm good." I spoon her, and she laces her small fingers with mine.

"I love you, CC."

The prickle behind my nose steals my words. I take a beat to recover before saying, "I love you, too, Maise."

"But there's just one thing . . ."

"What is it?"

"I get scared in this old house when Daddy's not here."

"Oh, you do?"

"Uh-huh."

"What can we do to fix that?"

"Well, there is one thing . . ."

"What's that?"

"When I'm scared, I sleep in Daddy's bed."

Oh.

Shit.

"Can we sleep in Daddy's bed, please, please . . . please."

She turns in my hold, and her hands are on my face. "He won't even know," she whispers.

"Hmmm, maybe just this once. I won't tell if you don't."

"Deal. But . . . I have my side, and you have to sleep on the stinky boy side."

"Um . . ."

"It's okay, you won't catch anything. My friend back in the city had a sleepover in Daddy's bed with me once and they woke up just fine."

I cackle out loud and Maisey giggles.

Okay, so we're doing this. I'm sleeping in Quinton's bed. Maise drags me from her bed by the hand, and we pad through the hall and into his room.

The second I cross the threshold, I'm hit with his sandal-wood and spice. And hell, I've never missed a person more than I do right now.

Maisey climbs into her side, and I slip into the other. When my head hits the pillow, I'm shrouded by his scent more so. The huge bed is soft and warm. And way too heady. My body has come alive just from the physical prox-imity to all things Quinton.

I ignore the tug of need, rolling over to focus on the brown eyes that are staring back at me. Maisey yawns, pulling the blankets up.

"Night, Maise," I whisper.

Her eyes stay closed. She really must be tired.

"Night, CC."

My eyes drift shut as sleep lulls me into its abyss . . .

I wake with a start. The dim light outlines a room that's vaguely familiar as it slowly comes into focus.

Quinton's room.

I turn to my right to find Maisey sound asleep.

Thank god.

I slip out of the bed and pad downstairs to check on things and grab a drink. I flip the light on and find a glass. Standing by the sink, I watch as the glass fills with cold water from outside. The glass cools as the waterline rises.

Shutting off the tap, I take a sip and lean on the counter. A moment later, the front door unlocks, and a disheveled man appears in the doorway.

EIGHTEEN

QUINTON

Celeste stands, hands by her side, lips parted around breathy inhales. The thin fabric of her long pajamas does nothing to cover her hard peaks.

"Everything okay?" I rasp.

I haven't slept a damn wink. I tried to sleep in the guest bedroom, but the mattress was like a rock. I, unlike Goldilocks, found the softest bed and fucking claimed it. It just so happened to be Celeste's bed. And despite its heavenly softness, I have been tossing and turning all damn night with her fragrance penetrating every single thing in that room.

If I wasn't hard before, I damn well am now.

She takes a step forward.

This time, we have no other distractions. But it's far too cold in this kitchen. I close the distance and sweep her into my arms. Her mouth is on mine a beat later. Walking to the living room, I set her down on the sofa. She pants where she sits, and I rekindle the fire until it's crackling away and the room is warming up rapidly.

"Quin . . ." she breathes.

I pad to where she sits and drop to my knees. "Fuck, CC. I've been tossing and turning in your bed for damn hours. Hell, I have blue balls from smelling you all night and not being anywhere near you. Not touching you."

"Not just me, then . . ."

Her eyes are ebony, consumed by need and the reflection of the flickering fire. Shadows dance over her face and neck. She's ethereal.

"Quin, please touch me," she begs.

No telling this man twice.

With deft fingers, I undo each button on her pajama top. And the lower I get, the slower my movements become. As if this moment is the one where we cross the line from fooling around to something far more serious.

After last night with Hank, my feelings for Celeste have amplified. Her dedication speaks volumes to the person she is.

When the last button pops, my hands drop to her sides, and I shift my focus up. Every heave of her chest has the shirt fall away a little more. Her hands move to mine, a finger tracing the back of my hand, like she too needs grounding in this intense parcel of time.

"Baby, I'm dying here, but I don't want to mess this up

by going way too fast." I drop my head into her lap. Instantly, her fingers rake through my hair.

"Me either," she whispers, cradling me as she bends down to dot a kiss into my hair.

Damn, it's been so long since I was on the receiving end of a woman's softness and affection. I'd forgotten how incredible it feels. And the need to return the feeling is overwhelming.

So much so, I rise, claiming her mouth. She slides forward on the sofa, closing the last of the space between us. Trailing my knuckles over her collarbone, I nudge the shirt from her, exposing one perfect breast. And damn if my mouth doesn't water like she's the first woman I've ever seen bare. Like she's not the finest fucking meal I'll ever have.

"I could fucking eat you alive," I growl, tracking hungry kisses down the soft column of her neck.

"Do it, Quin," she pants.

I will. I fucking will, but we're taking this slow, remember.

My throat all but closes over with the need lining her voice. "Slow, remember."

Fine hands tug at my shirt. "Off, please."

"So fucking polite. Is this all I had to do to get your sweet side?"

Her mouth brushes over mine, little panty puffs caressing my skin as she nips my bottom lip. That's all it takes to unleash the caveman in me. A low rumble rattles up my throat as I dip my head and clamp my mouth around a nipple.

A breathy gasp, "oh fuck," escapes as she arches, her head falling back.

Heat roars through my body, and I'm hard as granite, my boxers barely containing my cock. Celeste's needy hands hunt for who knows what as she opens further for me.

Fingers curl around my throat before they fall away, brushing over the tented fabric of my boxers a second later.

I release the peak with a pop, and brown eyes stare down at me on my knees for this stunning woman. I could spend every damn night with my knees pressed into the hardwoods if she'd let me.

"These pants are an abomination, baby. They're coming off."

She wriggles, lifting her hips as I tug the winter pajama pants over her ass and down her thighs. Taking each leg out in turn, I toss the pants on the end of the sofa. When I turn back, her shirt is draped over the hand she's holding out. Her dark eyes burn into mine.

And I'm fucking breathless.

Chest heaving, I slide the shirt from her fingers and toss it to the end of the sofa as well.

In only panties, she sits studying my face, as if at any moment I'm going to change my mind.

Not damn likely, woman.

"Look at you, CC." I tilt my head, letting my eyes shutter closed in an effort to stem the racing need threatening to have me blow my load in my boxers before I even get a taste of her.

Hell, that doesn't help.

Dammit, it's been way too long.

When fine fingers wrap around my jawline and her lips brush over my own, I open my eyes.

"Slow, okay?" she breathes.

"Yeah," I rasp.

My head is tilted up as her mouth crashes to mine. Arms aching to hold her, body alive with the burn for her I can barely restrain, I meet her hunger with my own.

A little whip of a whimper spills from her lips to mine.

Fuck.

Pushing to my feet without breaking the kiss, I sweep her off the sofa and onto my hips. Peaks pressed into my chest, she tightens her legs around my waist. I weave my hands through her hair, desperate to have her closer. A little moan from CC and my hand sinks, cupping a breast, my thumb whispering over her nipple.

Her hips roll, back arching a little as she breaks from the kiss. "Fuck, Quin . . ."

"More, baby?"

I pinch the nipple, and she's all but writhing in my hold. Turning a little, I kneel with one leg on the sofa and lay her down. When I release her and move down the sofa, she whimpers, "No, don't let go."

"Not letting you go, I promise."

I dot kisses over her collarbone, taking bites of her delicious, soft breasts as I drift over one then the other. Her hands crawl through my hair, her thighs falling apart at the same moment she moans, the movements coming together like a fucking symphony.

Gripping her hips, I work my way down her skin until I'm nipping the soft flesh of her inner thighs. Fingers slip away from my hair, curling around the fabric of the sofa. Her panties are soaked. I run a finger over the edge where the lacy material meets her thigh. "I did this to you, Celeste?"

"Uh-huh," she pants.

"Fuck, luckiest man alive."

"Qu—"

I slip a finger underneath the band to find silky velvet skin slippery with need.

I groan, letting the sound rumble through my chest and past my lips. Fuck, I am starving for this woman. More so than anyone I've ever met.

"These are coming off."

Worry twists her face as her tongue pokes out, wetting her lips. And when her bottom lip disappears between her teeth, I tug the panties over her hips. She lifts off the sofa, her legs trembling as I dispose of the last thing between us.

She closes her legs, looking up at the ceiling. Her chest rises and falls in shallow, snappy movements.

"Celeste, look at me," I rasp.

She shakes her head, pursing her lips.

"Baby, you're fucking stunning. And I'll die a slow and

painful death if you don't let me between these pretty thighs soon."

"I don't know . . ."

"Which part?"

"All of it . . . some of it?" She winces.

"Tell you what. I'll take my time, real slow, and you tell me when to stop. Okay?"

"A-alright."

"Open these sweet thighs, CC. Let me in."

They fall open and her hands cover her face instantly.

No fucking way.

I drag her hands from her face. "Eyes on me, or this ends now."

A whimper puffs from her as she shifts her gaze to my face.

"Good girl."

I move back a little more and dot kisses on the inside of her thigh, not breaking eye contact.

She's tense. Strung out tight, but for all the wrong reasons.

"Breathe, Celeste. Let me make you feel good. You deserve that and more."

"Okay," she utters.

I press her thighs open a little further. The one near the edge of the sofa slips off. I take it in my hand, resting her leg over my shoulder.

"Oh my god," she whines, tilting her head up so her gaze is anywhere but on me.

I nip the inside of her thigh. "Eyes on me, remember."

Slowly, her head drops. Her eyes, pupils blown out so wide her gaze is almost black, meet mine.

"Anything you don't like, tap my shoulder."

She nods.

Now I take a moment to take her in. She's bare. Her perfect, bare pussy glistens. And fuck, a man has never needed something this much.

Instead of devouring her straight up like I'm dying to do, I drop kisses to the top of her apex, letting a finger trace the sides of her entrance.

"Quin, oh . . ."

"More, baby?" I snap my head up, absolutely aware of my cruelty in denying her the touch where she wants it now.

But I want her to feel every single thing.

I want her to need my touch.

Crave it.

Need me.

Crave me.

"Eyes on me," I say, sweeping a finger through her entrance. Her hands leave the sofa, sinking into my hair. Her thighs fall open further.

Much better.

This time, when my mouth meets her pussy, I run my tongue through her glistening entrance. The second I get my first taste of her, my balls are tightening, my cock impossibly hard. I drop my forehead to her hip. *Fuck.* At this rate, I'm going to blow my load before she has a chance to come around my fingers.

"Quin?" She pushes up on the chair, panting.

"I'm good. It's just been a while, and yo—"

My breath vanishes.

Fuck.

Her hands find my face, lifting it until my gaze finds her. "Your eyes are . . ."

I'm guessing my pupils are dilated as fuck. "Just drunk on the taste of you, CC."

"Oh . . ." A ghost of a smile plays over her lips. "Well, in that case," she says, releasing my face, "as you were."

I chuckle. She always surprises me in the best way possible. Not wanting to waste a single moment of our stolen time together, I duck my head, planting a kiss over her swollen clit.

The throb coursing through it drums against my lips.

I kiss it again before sending my tongue around it. I grip her hips tight.

CC writhes on the sofa, back arching as she moans through parted lips.

"Still more, beautiful?"

"Don't you dare stop, MacKelvie."

I slide two fingers inside her tight, wet heat. When her back leaves the sofa, I clamp my teeth around her sweet little nub.

"Oh fuck," she pants.

Her pussy quivers, tightening around my fingers. I

pump them slowly, in and out, as I suckle her. Drawing out the pleasure from Celeste is a newfound pastime that will never get old.

She's been beautiful since the day we met, but right now, she's stunning.

Nothing will ever top the way she looks impaled on my fingers.

Well . . . maybe.

I can only imagine how fucking incredible she'd look riding my cock. Or manhandled in my rough grip while I fuck her, wild and desperate . . .

Oh fuck.

I suck down hard on her clit and pick up my pace when she starts to moan. A moment later, I'm rewarded, my name chanting through her lips as she milks my fingers, hips bucking off the sofa.

Losing contact for a beat, I say, "Good girl. Come all over my fingers, CC."

She does what she's told, riding my hand, bucking against my mouth as she teases out the orgasm.

And damn, I thought I needed her before . . .

When she catches her breath, she sits up, kissing my mouth.

Her hand falls to my stomach before her finger slides beneath my waistband.

"Tell me what you need, Quinnie. Please, I want to return the favor. Now I'm the one dying to taste."

Big brown eyes hold my gaze as she slips from the sofa to her knees.

CHAPTER

NINETEEN

CELESTE

The second my knees meet the hardwoods, I'm on fire again. Quinton strains against his Santa boxers, chest heaving, eyes darkened and homed in on my face. Disheveled and every inch of his body taut, he's gorgeous. I giggle at the tiny Santas on his pajamas asking if I've been naughty or nice.

Sorry Santa, I may have been nice, but I'm about to ruin that.

"Celeste . . ." His voice is gravel over deep and desperate inhales as his hands slide into my hair.

I slide the boxers down, releasing his cock. His shallow breaths peter out altogether.

I sweep the boxers down his legs, and he steps out.

I rest on my heels and take him in. His hands fall to his sides, and when I look back up to him, I swear he's stopped breathing.

Rising off my heels and back to my knees, I grip the base of his cock, keeping eye contact. His eyelids shutter closed, and his palms cup my face. "Fuck, woman."

The smile stretching my face feels so damn good. How long has it been since Quin had someone to take care of him? He spends every spare minute working or being with Maisey.

Something snaps in my chest as I realize I want to be the one to give him what he needs.

I trace the tip of my fingers around the head of his cock, eliciting a shudder. A drop of pre-cum beads at the tip.

"Cele—"

I slide him into my mouth.

The following groan is enough to wake the house.

How long has it been, Quin?

I slide over his length in long, languid strokes, keeping my eyes on his gorgeous face as it falls apart bit by bit. When his hands tighten around my face, it's the only warning I get before he takes over.

"Sorry, baby. It's either this or fuck you on the sofa," he rasps.

I shake my head to say it's fine.

I want him to have what he wants.

His pace quickens, sinking further into my mouth. Tears burn behind my eyes, and I clamp around him, sucking hard to fight off my gag reflex.

"Ah, fuck . . ." His grip turns punishing in my hair.

My hands wander his thighs, tracking to his balls. I roll

them through my fingers, and his head falls back on a low moan.

Good.

When his movement turns messy, I take up the rhythm and his gaze finds mine again.

"Bab—"

I tap my cheek, and his eyes all but roll back in his head.

I'll take it all, if he'll give it to me.

But when his gaze returns, it's desperate. It's like . . .

Hot release floods my tongue and I swallow it down—every wave he gives me.

Quin stills, his hands planted on my face. And I lose his cock from my mouth. Rough hands haul me to my feet a moment later, then strong arms have me off them. He sinks into the sofa, and I curl up in his lap.

"Fucking hell, CC," he whispers into my hair.

"Yeah" is all I can say.

His chest is still heaving. He wraps himself around me, dotting kisses down my neck and over my shoulder.

Embers bloom in my core with every hot, heady kiss that brushes my skin.

And I—

I turn on his lap, sinking my knees into the cushions either side of his thighs. "Quin." My hands find his jawline, his blues meet my gaze, and warm palms guide my mouth to his.

We weren't going to . . . but I . . .

I swallow hard.

God, all I want right now is him. Is us.

Breaking away, he brushes a strand of wayward hair behind my ear, blue eyes studying my face. "God, you're beautiful, Celeste."

I huff a breath. "Back at you, sweet man."

He slides a hand behind my neck, guiding my head down, pulling my forehead to his. "I don't usually do this type of thing. I can't let Maise get attached if—"

"I know. I mean, I understand . . ."

I pull away, forcing a smile. Does he regret what we just did?

I don't. Not at all.

He growls. "Where are you going?"

"I don't want to make things hard."

"Bit late for that," he says, glancing down.

I huff a laugh. "You know what I mean."

He clears his throat. "Yeah, I do."

"What about Maise?"

"She's asleep. We have"—he glances at the clock over the mantle—"at least two more hours."

"Hmmm, how shall we spend the—" A yawn drowns out the words.

He chuckles. "Asleep. I think we should spend them sleeping."

Crashing down from the high, I'm exhausted. Quin rises, taking me with him. I'm on wobbly footing a beat later as he helps me into my pajamas. He slips his boxers on before sweeping me into his arms like I weigh nothing.

Padding up the stairs, he presses kisses into my hair as I rest my head against his chest, trying and failing to stifle another yawn. He turns for Maisey's room.

"Other way, Quinnie."

"Hey? You two huddled up in my bed?"

I nod, the yawn slipping past my defenses.

"If I'd known you were in my bed, I would have been over here much sooner," he whispers.

I can't fight the thrill of excitement his words have traveling over my skin and through my body. But it fades when another yawn hits.

"Baby, I'm sorry I kept you up."

My eyes fall shut without my permission, my head lolling. "I'm not . . ." The words are barely words. The second they're out, Quin's warmth disappears, only to be replaced by the softness of his bed.

He tucks me in the way he does Maisey. Snug as a bug in a rug.

I try to laugh, but it's more like a dying moose noise as I roll over and snuggle down. Footsteps pad around the bed. I can barely crack one eye open, but it's enough to see him lean down to his daughter and plant a kiss into her hair. "Love you, kiddo."

She mumbles, rolling away from him, but he re-tucks her in.

My heart's a puddle inside my rib cage.

He's back on my side before I can process the sweetness that is this rugged, flannel-clad, burly man. Another kiss drops to my cheek. "See you in the morning, baby," he rasps.

Maisey rolls over with a whine. "I'm not a baby, Daddy," she mumbles.

He chuckles, planting more kisses to my hair before leaving.

I set down Dad's breakfast tray and wait while he takes his medication. "Get some sleep, Hank?"

"Mhmmm, a little." He swallows a mouthful of tea, plucking up a triangle of toast smothered in jam. It's always been his favorite breakfast—strong tea with a little milk, one sugar; two slices of strawberry jam on grain toast. He's a creature of habit, always has been.

"Good, well. Take it easy today, okay?"

He looks up at me now, his gaze snagging on the small Band-Aid I swapped the large bandage out for this morning. "You alright? What happened to your face?"

"Just being clumsy, is all. Finish your breakfast, and holler if you need me."

"Right, yes. Thank you for the tray." His gaze is anywhere but on me now, like it's impolite to stare at a stranger's woes. That part of my dad is still alive and well, I see.

I pad upstairs to my room. The bed is made, the place neat as a pin. Better than I left it.

Still tired from the last twenty-four hours, I flop onto my bed face-first.

I'm hit with the overwhelming scent of Quin.

I groan into the pillow.

Dammit. Why is he so damn addictive? I'm not so naive as to believe whatever we have between us will turn into something worth keeping. He has Maisey to think about. I may not be around for that long . . . If Dad gets worse, like he was last night, I will have no choice but to find a place for him in a home.

The devastating thought crashes into me.

Emotion closes over my throat.

Could I do that? Send him away, like a naughty kid who keeps messing up?

He would never give up on me. Ever.

But I can't take care of him properly here, or by myself, if he's—

I sob into the pillow. Ugly, long wails that break my heart inch by inch with every one that slips up my throat.

The first sign of trouble, and I'm just giving up.

I can't even be a decent daughter. How the hell would I cope with being responsible for someone for eighteen years . . . Like Quin is for Maisey.

I'm a hopeless daughter; I'd be an even worse parent.

I can't breathe.

The hot, damp pillow slowly suffocates me. My lungs

burn, and I snap my head up, pushing away from the bed with my palms.

I suck in much-needed cool air before crashing back down on my side and curling into a ball.

I've lost the plot. It was one incident, and Dad is fine. I'm the one who has a cut-up face.

Quin never asked me to be . . . anything. For him *or* Maisey.

I'm overreacting, overtired, and—ugh—just so over it.

I let the weight of the last month take me down, and it's not productive.

Time to get up and shower, and maybe eat then take a nap. The world will look brighter when I'm rested.

That's it, I'm just tired.

I haul my ass off the bed and into the shower. When I'm thoroughly warmed all the way down to my bones and utterly relaxed, I dress and pad downstairs to the kitchen. I make coffee and a slice of toast. Deciding to eat in my room to save any more questioning over my face, I walk back up.

Safe inside my room, I sit on the edge of my bed and eat my toast, taking sips of coffee.

With each one, the day seems brighter.

See, just needed to get myself sorted. A little hot water, a little coffee.

Placing the plate on my bedside table, I lay on the bed and roll onto my side. The pillow still smells like Quin. I don't know why I thought it wouldn't. But it catches me by surprise again, regardless.

Letting my eyes fall shut, I drown out every bad thought rattling around my head with memories of early this morning. In the living room . . . on the sofa by the fireplace.

I fall into the abyss of sleep before Quin gets to the good part.

Banging downstairs has me flying off the bed and down the stairs.

Something smashes as I round the end of the stairs and follow the noise to the sunroom. When I make it to the brightly lit room on the eastern side, furniture is upturned and the few potted plants that anchored the corners of the room are tipped over, the plants pulled from their oversized ceramic pots.

Shit.

Shit, shit, shit, shit.

Dad is stalking across the room, hands in his hair as he hunts for something. The urge to help flares. But self-preservation overrides it when he turns and spots me hovering in the doorway.

Fear snakes down my spine, making me nauseous the second it registers.

This is my *father*.

He's my dad, not some psycho maniac . . .

But right now, as he takes a step toward me, I can't tell the difference. I slide my hand to my back pocket to grab my phone.

I need Quin.

The pocket's empty.

Fuck.

CHAPTER
TWENTY
QUINTON

Maise is dancing around to Christmas carols, the volume so loud I can barely hear myself think. Luckily, we're about to head out. I have to help the crew with the last day of cleanup and pack up at the inn job.

"Maise! Turn it down, kiddo. We got to go in ten."

She's dancing, arms in the air, to some upbeat Christmas tune that would surely turn anyone who wasn't already deaf off Christmas altogether.

When she keeps spinning, belting out the chorus in her high, lilting tone, I zip the lunch bags up and shoulder my backpack before padding to the speaker. I hold a finger on the power button, and the noise snaps out instantly.

Maisey turns on me, a frown plastered over her pouty little face, hands on her hips. "Daddy! I was in the middle of something!"

A crash from next door sees us both turn toward the noise.

Fuck.

"Stay here," I growl out, flying through the front door. Barefoot, I plow through the snow toward CC's front door.

Something smashes against a wall as I come up against their locked door. I pound a fist into the wood, rattling the wreath Maise insisted on hanging last week.

I get no response, just more crashing.

Hell.

I round the house, and what I find when I make it to the oversized windows of the sunroom flips my gut, sending heat through my veins. The room is trashed.

And vacant.

Dammit, Hank.

I try the sunroom door, but it too is locked. I back up a step and kick it in. My steel caps thunder down the hall as I head toward the racket further inside the house.

"Celeste! Where are you?" I peer into each doorway I pass—the guest bedroom, the TV room, the living room.

"Who the fuck are you?" Hank appears in the hallway, coming from the kitchen.

No, not again.

I hold my hands up, trying to look as unintimidating as possible. "I live next door, Hank. I just came to see if you're okay, bud."

He all but snarls at me. "I'm not your bud. I don't even

know you. Agnes lives next door, so who the hell are you?" His hands ball to fists by his sides.

Agnes. My grandmother.

Fuck, this meltdown of Hank's is worse than I thought.

"I'm her grandson, Hank. Staying with her for a while." I decide to play along to avoid enraging him further.

"Never heard of you!" He picks up a vase on the hallway side table and tosses it at my head. I duck sideways, and it shatters the second it connects with the wall, shards raining onto the hardwood floor.

All I can think of is getting to Celeste.

But she'll have my balls for baubles if I hurt her father to get to her. Too damn selfless for her own good, that little woman.

I take a step toward the kitchen.

"Don't come any closer, or . . ." Hank tilts his head, gaze tightening like he means business.

Which he fucking does.

"I just want to make sure Celeste is alright. *Please.*"

His face blanks.

"Please, Hank, let me past."

"I don't know who you're dribbling about, boy. Me and Tisha are in the middle of something here. And it ain't none of your business."

The fuck?

"I know you don't want to hurt her. I just want to check she's okay. Come on, Hank."

But he doesn't back down, stepping into my space now. "Why is another man coming to check up on my wife, hey?"

Oh geez.

"I'm just a friend, nothing more."

"I don't believe you, sonny." He swings.

I catch his arm and bend it behind his back. He crashes to his knees, crying out. My hold on him almost slips when he fights back. He's surprisingly strong for an old guy.

"Calm down, Hank. Nobody is here to hurt anyone."

"Quin," a small voice quivers from the kitchen doorway. Celeste's tear-stained cheeks are reddened under watery eyes. "Please don't hurt him."

"You know I won't. Call the paramedics. Tell him he's had another episode."

"M-my phone's upstairs."

"It's okay. We'll wait." I nod to the stairs.

She takes them two at a time on wobbly legs. When she returns, she's already speaking to someone, small sobs escaping between each answer she gives. By the time she hangs up, Hank's relaxed in my hold. His eyes flicker up to his daughter, and I witness the moment he realizes what he's done. Again.

"Celeste . . ." His voice breaks.

"I'm okay, Daddy. The paramedics are going to come and help, okay?" She kneels in front of him, their eyes level. "Maybe they can just adjust your medication, you know. So you don't get so confused and upset?"

Hank shakes his head, but he's tense in my hold again.

We wait with bated breath for the ambulance. And when the brakes squeal on the slushy street outside, CC runs for the door to let them in.

I don't let go until the medics have given him a sedative. And the second the paramedics have Hank safe and taken care of, I haul Celeste into my arms.

An onslaught of sobs crashes into my chest as they place Hank onto a gurney and wheel him out into the ambulance.

"He needs an assessment, Celeste. He'll be okay. Possibly his condition has outgrown his medication. The docs will have him sorted, I promise."

Fingers curl around my now-damp shirt.

When the ambulance drives back down the street, I hold CC at arm's length. "You did so fucking good by him, baby. Please don't think any of this is your fault."

Her face breaks, and I just know she is blaming herself for this.

"I got to get back to Maise and then to work. Will you be okay, or do you want to tag along?"

She wipes her face, looking around the trashed house. "I should clean this up."

"Leave it. I'll help you when I get home."

"It's fine, I can do it. I need to keep busy, anyway. And tagging along will probably just end up with me being in your way. I don't want to be a hassle."

I trace a finger over her temple, brushing a damp strand of dark hair behind her ear. "Baby, you are never a hassle.

You got that? You need me—hell, even just want to hang out and someone to talk to—I'm right here."

She nods, rolling her lips together.

I dot a kiss to her forehead and spend a few minutes righting the heavy items back on their feet before telling her I'll check in later. Pulling the sunroom door to the backyard closed, I make a mental note to fix the broken latch when I get home.

When I push through the front door to our house, I find Maise pacing, arms folded, face pinched with worry. "Is CC okay?"

She flies into my arms.

"Yeah, kiddo. She's okay."

"Then it was Hank in the ambulance?"

"It was. Grab your coat. We're late."

We pile into the truck and head for the inn. The instant I climb out of the truck, Caleb is in my face.

"Is Celeste okay? We heard Hank's in custody."

Holy hell, they weren't wrong about the small-town grapevine.

"Hank is getting his meds adjusted, hopefully. Maybe some respite. There were no handcuffs involved, Caleb. Where on earth did you hear that from?"

Caleb's sheepish expression turns to the inn's front door, where Helen from the front desk stands waiting.

"Ah, I see you're getting your intel from a reliable source, at least," I deadpan.

"Yeah. Shit, sorry. Should have known better than to

believe a word the Grafton grapevine had to say." He throws Helen an annoyed look. She tilts her nose up, rolls off the doorframe, and stalks inside.

I help Maise out of the truck, and we get to work. Double-checking every part of the renovation, I walk the jobsite like I would any big build and triple-check all the small details. Maise follows behind, listening and asking the boys if they have done this or done that.

Mostly it gets laughs out of them. Until she catches a mistake or an imperfection.

"Maise, can you grab some sodas from the cooler in the back seat of the truck?" I ask.

"Sure, Daddy." She skips off, heading for the truck parked by the entrance.

"See the boss lady has you all sorted out today," Caleb says with a chuckle.

"It's been a weird morning. First I was sassed for turning off some abomination of a Christmas song by my five-going-on-fifteen-year-old daughter. Then the whole Hank thing. To add insult to injury, I left Celeste alone after . . ."

"Fuck, man, you could've stayed. We have this covered." He frowns.

"Maybe. Besides, it's my job to double-check, not yours. It's my reputation on the line."

"Ah, true." He slides a screwdriver into his back pocket and rifles through the hardware box until he comes up with another antique brass fitting. Installing it, he looks back at me. "You know, we all love Hank and CC. But old Mr.

Black has been struggling for a while. Before Marie left, he was starting to muck up in town. That's why she stopped taking him out."

"Seriously?"

"Yeah, he was bad. Always ripping his clothes off. Getting aggressive with folks for no reason. At least it looked that way, anyway. I was surprised when Marie left CC in charge. If anything, that man needs more help. Marie kind of did the dirty on CC. And I'm guessing by what happened this week, CC had no idea."

"Fuck." I swipe my hand through my hair. "Let's hope they keep him in the hospital a while. It isn't fair to CC. And you're right, he needs more help than just a live-in caretaker. Much more."

"Guess someone will figure that out. None of our business, I suppose."

I chuckle. "Says Mr. Grafton Grapevine."

He just shrugs, returning his focus to the hardware in his grip. I grab a few pieces from the box and get to fitting them. With most of my checks done, I need to keep my hands busy.

"Here, Daddy." Maise hands me a soda. "Can you open mine?"

"Sure, kiddo. But only half, alright?"

"Uh-huh . . ." She's nodding, but somehow I don't believe her.

My back pocket buzzes, and I slip my screwdriver between my teeth and pull the phone out.

Thank you for this morning. 🩶

Damn, CC.

This little woman has gone far too long without someone on her side. Someone to always root for her.

Anytime, baby. You know where I live. 😙

I do. 🩶

That simple response has my face stretching in the most ridiculous smile. It feels out of place after this morning. But drama aside, I can't help but notice how every day we grow so much closer. Maybe it's too soon. We've only known each other weeks. Three, to be exact . . .

But if the intensity of those three weeks was weighted accordingly, it would be more like months.

And what I wouldn't give for months with Celeste.

Even years.

Maise walks the room, hands on her hips like she's the boss, not her old man. And the way the guys play the part in her little charade is heartwarming.

Ronan strides over, packing away the tools as Caleb and I install the last few pieces of hardware. "Place is looking stellar, boss man."

"Tidied up pretty nicely, I reckon." I let my gaze wander over the finished dining room. We did good. And just in the nick of time.

Miranda saunters in. "Oh, packing up already?"

"All done. All it needs now is a final inspection." I wave my hands toward the renewed space. She takes a turn around the large old room looking over every section of it, like she hasn't been here the entire time we've been on the job. When she spins back with a smile, hope blooms. "Very nice, Quinton. And on time, too. At this rate, we'll have you fixing up the rest of the place before long."

"Any work you can send our way is welcome, Miranda."

Her smile widens. "I'm sure there is plenty of that."

Maybe this small-town thing will work out, after all.

CHAPTER

TWENTY-ONE

CELESTE

My leg jumps on the spot, jostling me in the hard plastic seat. The anxiety-ridden bouncing earns me a filthy look from the older woman in the seat beside mine at Grafton General Hospital.

"Black?" A nurse walks out with a clipboard, looking around the room above our heads like they always do.

"Here!" I shoot off the seat like it's made of hot coals. And she wastes no time leading me to the family room. Inside sits my father and who I presume is the doctor.

"Miss Black, how are you this morning?" the doctor asks, a shallow smile on his face. I glance at Dad and give him a soft smile.

He stares back, pushing up a polite nod of the head, as if a stranger just walked in with room service. Someone he'll never see again but can't bring himself to be impolite to.

221

I replay the doctor's question in my mind. *How are you? Do you really want to know?*

It's only been two days since my father left with the paramedics, and the guilt is eating me alive. I've barely slept. Every conversation I have with my sister and brother end the same way. And there have been at least five of those with either of them, and a group video call that went sideways way too quick. They don't want Dad in a home.

Nor do I, but . . .

Then there was the night I spent at Quin's the first time. And I swear, now that I've had time to process everything, he was just trying to help by distracting me.

"I'm fine." I sit on the chair, trying not to let my gaze stick to my father.

"Good, good. Let's get started, shall we?" he asks Dad this time.

"Whatever you say, Doc." Dad raises his hands in assent before resting them on his thighs.

"So we have had a chance to reassess the medications as well as observe." The doctor nods as if questioning my understanding.

"Yes, and?" I reply.

"We have made some alterations, which should make life a little easier. Less incidents related to aggression and so on, at least. The medication does take a few days to take effect, and we always monitor each person carefully when starting a medication like this before we send them home. So Hank will be staying another few nights with us. Then, if all goes to plan, he can go home. We've already had this discussion with Hank, so, how does that sound to you?"

"Um, good, I guess. What happens if it doesn't work?"

"That isn't usually a problem. But in the rare case that he doesn't respond to the medication, we would try an alternative route."

"Oh, okay."

All of this is over my head.

His demeanor is . . .

He just keeps talking about Dad like he's not even here.

"Great!" He slaps his thighs, and I jump in the seat.

"That's it?" I ask, glancing to Dad, who's staring out the small window instead of being part of a conversation that is about him.

"Yes, was there something else?" The doctor stands, adjusting his lab coat.

"No, I guess not."

He waves a hand toward the door, and I rise from the chair. Dad sits rooted to the spot, oblivious to the doctor and me leaving.

"Sandy will be back for your—Hank shortly. I'll see you in two days. Sandy will book you in for then."

He disappears from the room, but I can't bring myself to leave. To just leave Dad in this empty room by himself, staring at nothing.

So I stay planted in the doorway until Sandy shows.

"Oh, hey. You must be Celeste. It's so lovely to meet you."

"Hi, likewise. How's he really doing?"

She gives me an empathetic smile. "Doctor Baron isn't the warmest man on the planet, but he's brilliant at his job." She stops beside me, folding her arms. "He's doing pretty good, all things considered."

"That's great," I say, but the words almost lodge in my throat.

She turns and rubs my arm. "This is the hardest thing you'll ever have to do, hon. Watch a loved one you've known your entire life fade away from you in slow motion. It's a real kick to the gut."

I scrunch my face up, trying to stem the tears piling up behind my eyes from falling.

"You are doing an incredible job, sweetheart. This kind of thing is heart-wrenching."

"You sound like you are talking from experience."

"My mom. She passed two years back, but the last five were really hard."

And just like that, nothing about our everyday feels as hard anymore. The thought of losing my father trumps any difficult moment.

"The best advice I can give you is to have someone, even if it's just one person, that you can call day or night if you need support. And—this last one is a must—do something for yourself every single day. If your cup is empty, there is no way you'll come out the other side of this, after giving everything day after day, and not need therapy if you don't take care of *you* regularly."

"I—"

"Don't forget those two, okay? They were literally my lifesavers."

I huff a strained breath. Quin, my person to call day or night, is my lifesaver. Dramatic? Maybe. True? One hundred percent, in so many ways.

"You take care, okay? And I will make sure he's well looked after."

"Thank you," I breathe.

"Of course. Now get out of here. Let me do my job." She winks at me as she walks to my father. "Hello again, Hank. Ready for a cup of tea and a chat, hon?"

"Oh, there you are. I was wondering when someone was coming to take me to the train station. I've been waiting right here for hours, and I can't be late. Tisha is waiting."

"No, we can't have that. Let's grab that tea first, hey?"

"Yes. Yes, tea is good."

I roll off the doorframe and wander back down the sterile hospital corridor. The small-town hospital is a general ward, housing a mix of patients. Each one with their own story, no doubt. And I can't help but notice how incredibly drab the place is.

And I know just the woman to bring some color to these old walls.

For the first time in two decades, the double doors to my mother's art studio under the big old oak in our backyard fall open. Dust and a light shower of snow falls from the doors as they creak around their hinges, letting light into the space that used to breathe with color and creativity.

The old wooden shed is drafty, the cold currents of air that wind through gaps in the boards playing with the dust and debris over the floor. Water damage has warped some spots of the shed's walls, and the two long tables that still hold all her supplies have split veneer.

The windows on every side are boarded up. Most likely by my father not long after we lost Mom. Still, his efforts only served to keep *us* out, not the weather. The whole space needs fixing or, at the very minimum, a lot of love.

Her old stool, the one that swivels with the padded seat, sits by the table at the end, next to a dust-covered easel. I pad to where it stands, lifting the cloth draped over it.

A half-finished landscape stares back at me.

And I feel the weight in my chest, as I do with every memory of my mom. This time, it's a little lighter. As if rediscovering her passion is a reunion of sorts for us. I run a fingertip over the oil-based paint, the texture uneven and abstract on my skin. "Hey, Mom," I whisper.

I remember as a teenager begging Dad to let me into the studio, wanting to see her paintings one last time. Now, being in here, I feel the overwhelming urge to clean up the space and give it new life. A way to honor her, I guess.

Something for her.

But something for myself, a space to work on my art and refill my cup. And even if nothing comes from it, at least I have my own version of respite.

That is, if I can get this old relic of a studio fixed up . . .

Outside, I study the boards over the windows. Crowbar or—

"Celeste!"

I spin around to find Maisey plowing through the snow at me. She launches herself into my arms, and I hug her tight, glad for her company.

"Where's your daddy, hon?"

She pushes back a little, her arms draped over my shoulders as her face breaks into a smile.

"He's right here," Quin says from behind, snow crunching as he crosses the yard at a steadier pace then his daughter did.

"Oh, hey. How was your job wrap-up?" I ask.

He tilts his head with a wry smile. "It was fine. How's your dad?"

Maisey wriggles and I pop her down onto her feet. "He's okay. A little better. Starting new meds, so hopefully that will help. They said he can come home in a few days, if the medication settles things."

"That's great . . ."

But his tone is far from relieved.

"This is his home, Quinton. Where he belongs."

He rubs a hand behind his neck with a wince.

I set my shoulders, folding my arms over my chest. "You don't—"

"CC . . ." He eliminates the distance between us. "You are the most selfless fucking woman on the planet, you know that? But Hank coming home might not be what turns out to be the best thing for him. Or you. Please just think about that, okay?"

"No." I'm shaking my head. "That's giving up on him, Quinton. I won't do it."

"No, it's not. Not if he needs more care than you're able to give. Not if it means you're not safe." His voice is laced with concern.

"I'm not talking to you about this. It's for me and my brother and sister to decide."

"I know that. But when they are thousands of miles away, expecting you to look after someone who needs more care than one person is capable of, who is going to look after *you*?"

The second the words leave his mouth, his face falls with something like shock. As if he just realized he over-stepped.

"I'm sorry for—"

I hold a hand up. "Just drop it, please."

Something tugs on my sweater, and I glance down to see

Maisey's face twisted with worry. "What do you mean nobody takes care of you, CC?"

Her brows pinch together even further, and my heart all but stalls out.

I bend down and give her a tight hug. "I'm just fine. Don't you worry about me, sweetheart. Besides, with you as my bestie, I'm the luckiest girl alive."

She scoffs, breaking from the hug. "You mean woman—luckiest *woman* alive. That's what Daddy calls you when he thinks I'm not listening. He said you're the stunning woman that just *had* to move in next door muddling up his head. That's what he said."

My mouth falls open. The annoyance I was feeling toward Quin just seconds ago ebbs.

Quinton looses a groan as his hand rubs down his face. "You gotta repeat everything I say, Maise?"

She giggles and runs off to play in the snow.

"So, I take it having a woman living next door wasn't on your vision board?" I ask with a chuckle.

"What the hell is a vision board?" he says.

"You know, where you put all your future dreams and plans?"

"Yeah, no. Don't have one."

"Maybe you should make one. Then you can stop talking to yourself."

He slaps my ass and I squeal, bursting into a sprint to get away from him.

He bends down and scoops up snow, making a ball

before tossing it in my general direction. It hits the trunk of the old oak, and I fly behind the studio, coming to rest as I lean on its weathered boards. The crunch of steel caps on snow lets me know he's almost found me. Offense is the best defense, so I gather up a snowball of my own and hold my hand up, ready to sling it at that handsome mug of his the second he finds me.

He steps closer and closer.

I ready my snowball . . .

TWENTY-TWO

QUINTON

Snow explodes all over my face. If it wasn't for the giggle that came from its point of origin, I'd think it was Maise. Except this particular voice, the sunshine lilt and tone, sends electricity through my veins.

Spark after delicious fucking spark.

Run, baby . . .

Maise intercepts me, a snowball flying at my head, which I only just duck and miss. I can see whose side she's picked. *Little traitor.*

I ball up another shot and send it flying into her back.

She spins around. "Hey, not fair!"

"Oh yeah? Two against one isn't fair, either, kiddo. But here we are."

She knows I'm joking but sticks her tongue out at me, anyway.

Something moves behind me, but I'm too slow. A hand

tugs at the back of my coat and ice slides down my back. "Jesus Christ, Mary, and Jose—"

CC runs across the snow, desperate to put space between us.

"Daddy! Language!" Maise screeches but topples over laughing as she and CC try to get away but slip and slide in a tangle of legs and hit the cold snow together.

I stalk to where they are lying in a heaving pile of giggles and feigned fear.

"Please have mercy on us! In our defense, it's more like almost one whole adult against . . . well, you." CC's eyes don't waver from my gaze.

I guess she has a point.

I extend a hand to help her up. Maise is already on her feet, hands loaded with snowballs.

When Maise narrows her eyes at me, I reach down to CC.

Her hand slides into mine. It's cold.

I haul her upward, but she drops her weight. I lose my footing, crashing onto the snowy ground beside her.

"That's better. Down here with me," she whispers into my ear.

Maise tilts her head, giving us an odd look before something like anticipation claims her expression.

CC jumps to her feet, and Maisey's look fades.

She was waiting for us to . . . ?

I grab CC's hand and haul her back down. This time, she lands in my lap.

Where she fucking belongs.

"What are you—"

I cup her face with my hands. "Think the cat is outta the bag, baby. But it's up to you."

Her gaze studies my face for a beat, then she glances at Maisey. "Are we putting it back in?"

I swallow hard. I don't fucking want to, but . . .

"It's up to you."

"Kiss her already, Daddy!"

We both burst out laughing as Maisey drops her snowballs to the ground, arms folding over her chest. *Yep, that'll make us cooperate, kiddo.*

"I don't want to start something we can't finish," CC mutters, gaze dropping to where our fingers are still laced together. "I can't do that to her, Quin."

That right there is the whole reason I know she is the woman I want in my life. Permanently.

"We'll just start small, hey?" I say, tucking a rogue strand of hair behind her ear.

"Small?"

"Yeah, small, slow. At least when we're in company."

"Okay, I can do that."

My hand brushes over her cheek, my thumb dragging on her bottom lip. Maise stands behind CC, still waiting, her hands now on her hips, looking like we're the petulant children and she's the not-so-patient parent.

"We should probably do as she asks," I rasp.

CC moves on my lap, and I can't wait a second longer. I palm her face, pull her mouth down to mine, and kiss her.

"Yes!" Maise whoops, dancing around in the snow. "I knew it!"

CC puffs a laugh against my lips before breaking away. "What have we done, Quin?"

I chuckle. "Get ready for the most intrusive relationship you've ever had, baby."

She drops her forehead to my shoulder. "I have a feeling it'll be worth it."

Four hours later, Maise is in bed. Finally. It took an hour and a half to get her ready and tucked in between six million questions about when CC and I are getting married and giving her a little sister, or what she should wear to the summer wedding. Because she hates the cold.

I sidelined most of those questions with a flakey response about grownups having to decide these things and earned myself at least a dozen eye rolls in the process.

"Night, kiddo." I pull her door shut.

"Night, Daddy," she calls out. "Night, CC!"

Celeste, who is downstairs wrapping gifts for her

siblings for the first time in years, calls up the stairs. "Night, hon."

And for the first time in my life, I feel like everything is right with the world. Everything is in its place. The people I love are—

I grip the doorknob, resting my head against the closed door.

Fuck.

That sure as hell crept up on me.

I'm in love with Celeste Black.

I try to rationalize it each step of the way back down, but by the time I make it to the living room, I can't reason away the intense feeling I have for the little woman sitting on my living room floor among wrapping paper, ribbon, and name cards under the sparkling strings of fairy lights around the room.

"Hey, Quinnie. Almost done. You need anything wrapped?" She looks up from the present she's working on.

I stop by the sofa, almost breathless at the sight of her in my house doing something so mundane, just living. A stone occludes my airway as I rasp, "I'm good."

"What's wrong?" She pushes to her feet and pads to where I stand. Her elegant fingers flatten my brow. I must have been frowning. "What's got you worried, hey?"

"Not worried, just . . ." I close the space between us and take her face in my hands, dotting a kiss on her forehead. "Content."

"Well, if that's your content face, I think it's broken." She nips my neck.

"Oh yeah, what about this one?" I haul in a lungful before meeting her gaze. And by the heat that's growing in my core and the blood that just rushed south with her touch, I'm guessing she'll read this expression much differently.

"That one's . . ." She nudges her nose along my jawline. "One of my favorites."

"Is that so?"

I brush my lips over hers, and she slides her hands around my neck and into my hair. "It is."

Her heartbeat thunders under my fingertips when my hands fall from her face, grazing her neck on the way to the buttons of her sweater. "Got a Christmas wish, baby?"

"Sure do." Brown eyes darken as she draws my mouth down to hers.

Hungry, I take everything she gives up, exploring and devouring. Her hand tugs at my button-down flannel, and I haul it off my back, leaving behind my T-shirt.

"What about Maise?" CC breathes, her forehead resting against mine.

"She'll be out like a light, but we can check on the way to my room, if you want."

"Please tell me your bedroom door locks."

"Absolutely it does. You sleeping over?"

Brown eyes search mine. "I want to, I really do."

I haul her onto my hips before she gets another word

out, taking the steps two at a time. We pass Maisey's room, and I crack the door to check she's asleep.

Out cold.

She's always been a good sleeper. Happens, I suppose, when you run at a mile a minute all damn day.

"Satisfied?" I ask.

She simply nods, her gaze snagged on my face. Her fingers explore my neck, hair, and every angle of my face on the way to my room.

My heart thunders under her scrutiny.

Will she like what she finds? Will we make this work?

And what happens to my heart, to Maisey's, if it doesn't?

Nope.

Past that point.

Life is full of risk. And damn, I haven't wanted a woman this way ever in my entire life. That has to mean something.

I close the bedroom door softly behind us and flick the lock. "Just you and me."

"Good." Her mouth meets mine the second the syllable leaves her lips.

I spin and pin her to the door.

She releases a little moan in my mouth, and I'm hard as fuck. Desperate for nothing between us.

Hands start tugging at my T-shirt. And I let her struggle for a little while I taste that sensitive spot beneath her ear, every inch of her soft neck, and then dip to her collarbone.

I don't let up until I have her writhing against the door.

"Qui—" A whimper tumbles from her as I nudge her chin up with my nose and mouth.

We are making this last.

"Too many clothes, baby."

This time, it's going to be bare, raw, and torturously slow.

At least, that's my plan.

I want to cover every inch. Taste every part of her. Find out what she likes. What she doesn't.

I let her down to her feet and am pulling her sweater over her head a beat later. I leave the shirt on, the silky button-down blouse sticking to her skin with static accentuating every curve, the roundness of her perfect damn breasts.

What I wouldn't do to have one of those in my mouth right now . . .

"Off, Quin. Take it off, please."

I ignore her, tracing the pad of my thumb over the hard peak pushing against the silky shirt and lacy bra underneath. I feel the intricate texture of the lace as I swirl my thumb around the nipple.

Celeste's head falls back against the door with a thud.

"We're going to have to move before you wake Maise up," I whisper, sweeping her into my arms. I place her in the center of the bed and step back, just taking in her lying on my bed for a minute.

"What?" she says, breathy and strung out.

"Just thinking you—"

Fuck.

My throat closes over. I've been a girl dad for too damn long. Every emotion Maise feels, I live through, rewiring my brain to the softer side of life. Where the precious things live.

One of those now lies splayed over my bed.

And I know a life-altering moment when I'm looking down at one.

"You sure, CC?"

She pushes up, her elbows digging into the mattress. "Very."

I crawl onto the bed, over CC, until our gazes are level. "Hey, baby."

Her hands slide across my jawline and into my hair. "Hey, Quinnie."

"Slow, remember," I breathe.

She nods. Her hands wander to her buttons, and she pops them one by one. "I can live with slow."

"Good to know."

The blouse falls away, and I capture one hard peak between my teeth.

"Get it off," Celeste gasps.

I slide a hand under her back, releasing the bra clasp. She hauls the lingerie off her chest and tosses it onto the floor. I dot kisses around her chest, ignoring her heaving peaks, knowing all too well she's desperate for me there.

One hand holds me above her while the other tracks over her stomach, brushing my knuckles over the soft skin. Goosebumps flourish along her belly following my touch.

And when she's all but breathless, I bend my head and pluck a taut nipple between my teeth.

She arches off the bed instantly on a whimper.

Fuck.

I don't know who's torturing who here.

My rigid cock strains against my jeans. And when a little mewl slips as I pop the hard peak from my mouth and take up the other, I all but need to fist my cock to stop from embarrassing myself.

The way this little woman flays me open, leaving me needy and vulnerable with a wordless syllable, is ridiculous.

The overwhelming need to bury myself as deep inside her as possible sends my head spinning.

I need to taste her.

To feel her tighten around me as she comes, taking me with her.

"Baby, I don't know if slow's going to work this time," I rasp.

No telling my girl twice. Her hands work my shirt from my back. She pushes off the mattress again, trailing kisses over my damn chest, her dark hair swinging around her shoulders.

When she makes it to my stomach, I tense, wanting to be the one to lay her bare first.

I grab her wrists when her hands move to my waistband.

"No, I'm fucking devouring you first."

She opens her mouth to object, but I flick the button on

her jeans and have the zipper down and the heavy fabric over her hips a second later.

She wriggles and I pull them off, losing them to the floor.

Her lacy panties are soaked. And so coming off.

I slide a finger behind the waistband of the panties and have them gone next. I strip down until we are both bare, not a stitch between us. Standing at the edge of the bed, I survey the most stunning damn woman I've ever seen.

"Fucking hell, Celeste. This pretty little pussy consumes my damn dreams. But it's never as good as the real thing. You're fucking glistening for me, baby."

"I—"

I don't give her a chance to respond, dropping to my knees and sliding my hands behind hers, hauling her to the edge of the bed. A little squeak slips past her lips, and my cock twitches.

I spread her wide.

Her hands turn to fists around my duvet.

"Come all over my face, Celeste."

I dive in, lapping at her clit and sending my tongue through her wet center. She's breathless, chanting my name softly a minute later. Her knuckles turn white, and I can feel her tensing. Legs trembling, she widens them. "Quin . . ."

"Yeah, baby."

"Fuck, more."

I suckle hard on her clit, slipping two fingers inside her tight pussy.

And it's all I can do not to make a mess of the damn duvet hanging over the bed. I pause—just for a moment—breathing deeply.

She opens willingly for me. Not shy and unsure like the first time we touched. She lets go so easily with me now. Fucking perfect.

We just fit.

I send my tongue around her nub before sucking down hard. She flies off the bed, hands sinking into my hair, her grip turning painful.

Those hands slip, tilting my head up, her fingers wrapped around my jaw. Her mouth crashes over mine before she breaks away. "No more, I want to come with you."

I crawl up onto the bed, taking her onto my hips. "Good fucking girl."

TWENTY-THREE

CELESTE

Quinton crawls onto the bed, collecting me up onto his hips as he goes. We're in the center of the mattress, me straddling his lap as he rocks back onto his heels. His mouth finds my peak, and *fuck*. My head falls back, eyes shuttering closed as pure bliss sinks into my chest.

"Quinnie," I rasp.

"Mhmmm." The sound reverberates between my rib cage, sinking somewhere deep.

"Do we need something?"

He loses the peak with a pop and looks up. "It's been over six years since I've . . . I'm clean, baby."

"Same. And I have an IUD, so . . ."

"Fuck, I so wanted you bare. Guess my Christmas wish is about to come true." The shit-eating grin on his face is melting my soul. Even more so when it fades to desperation.

I can't wait a second longer.

I line the tip of his cock to my aching, soaked entrance. "Then make *mine* come true already, will you?"

He grabs my hips, stalling my movements. "And what exactly does this Christmas wish entail, Celeste?"

"You, me. On every surface we can find."

He drops his forehead to my chest with a groan. "You are literally fucking perfect, woman."

I loose a huffy chuckle and wriggle in his hold, wanting to lower down.

"Uh-uh. In a minute. There's no rush." His blues are dark. The brush of his tip against my entrance is blissful torture. All I want is to feel him inside me.

And there absolutely is a rush on this, Quinton.

I'm burning up alive here.

"Come on," I whisper. "Give in to me, sweet man."

He grunts, the sound straining as his throat bobs. His eyes close as his grip on my hips fades.

Threading my fingers through his hair, I dot kisses over his neck before my lips brush against his ear. "Let go, Quinnie."

His eyes drift open and his jaw feathers. "On one condition."

I peck his lips, hands grasping his jawline as I utter, "What's that?"

"Let me love you the way you deserve, Celeste."

And . . . heavens above. *That* I didn't expect. Emotion

steals the air in my lungs, prickles blooming behind the bridge of my nose.

Knuckles brush over my cheek as Quin's gaze holds mine. The second his hand leaves my face, it reaffirms on my hip.

And I'm slammed down.

He thrusts up, sinks up to the hilt, and leaves my empty lungs starved on a choppy gasp.

"Fucking hell, baby," he growls, holding me motionless as we both adjust, heaving through each desperate breath. "Dammit, don't you move. Give me a second."

I'm so tempted to wriggle all over his lap, but I don't want to ruin this moment. Don't want to be responsible for ending this too soon. And the stretch, the overwhelming size of him is sending my head spinning.

The last thing I want to do is move.

Tightness seizes my chest, an ache growing as I realize the line we've crossed. The depth and velocity of what lies between us after just three short weeks.

And it must be etched all over my face . . .

"Breathe, baby." Quin's hands cup my face. "It's just you and me."

I nod, but the oxygen seems to have evaporated from the room.

"Celeste, we can stop. You tell me, and we stop."

How badly I want to tell him it's me, not him. It's my bundles of insecurities, history of bad decisions, and inability to see things through that haunt me in this moment. This moment that should be beautiful, freeing, and just between us.

"Baby, you gotta talk to me," he rasps.

"I—"

I draw in a shuddering breath, and the slight motion has him twitch inside me. Lighting me up from the inside like nothing before.

Hands grip my face. "Beautiful, you're scaring me. I need to know what's going on in this head of yours."

"I don't . . . I can't—" I close my eyes briefly before studying his face. "It's only been three weeks, but I feel— you feel like . . ."

I'm terrible at this stuff. Always have been.

"I feel like what?" he says softly.

"Home." The word breaks, and the relief that floods his face has my own bunching up as tears swell.

Shit.

"God, baby, I had no idea how much I was missing until you showed up in this tiny little town. Now I don't think I can go without."

Mostly recovered from the realization of who this man is to me, I try my luck and wiggle my hips, just a little bit.

"Ah, fuck," he groans.

"I really want to move," I whisper.

His head ducks as he plucks a nipple through his teeth. "Mhmmm."

I take the initiative and rise on my knees a little. My

mouth falls open as I feel every inch of him. Teeth tighten around my peak, a groan slipping past his lips.

"Qui—"

My back meets the bed, and the air puffs from my chest. Rough hands haul my hips upward toward his, and he has me spread wide. One deep, incredible thrust, and he's sunk to the hilt again. "Fuck, CC . . . You're tight, so fucking wet, and goddamn *mine*."

Every punishing thrust has my pussy clenching tighter around him. The way this man goes from sweet and sensitive to demanding and filthy-mouthed is a delight.

And I'm so here for it.

"God, we are incredible. You take my cock so fucking well, Celeste."

He brushes a thumb over my clit, and I arch off the bed, shoulders digging into the mattress. I clamp down around his cock, unable to stall the imminent orgasm building.

"Not yet, beautiful."

He slows his pace, his thrusts growing more shallow as I writhe on the bed in annoyance.

"Quin, please."

"No."

My mouth gapes. Now he's just being the orgasm grinch. *Ass*.

But to my surprise, he leans down, letting my hips lower to the bed, my back pressing into the mattress. "We have all night. We're not rushing the best part."

Crawling over me, he takes up a rhythm, slow and deep. Kisses find my neck, my breasts, and that hollow spot where my throat meets my collarbone. My hands wander through his hair as he tracks kisses around the soft flesh of each breast before sucking on a hard peak.

And the tight coil of an orgasm builds once again.

I slide a hand to my clit, letting my fingertips dance over the sensitive bud. A moan slips past my lips, and he notices where my hand is.

His harsh grip has my wrists pinned to the bed above my head a second later. "Determined to get on that naughty list, aren't you, beautiful?"

I huff a sound that's noncommittal. "I have no idea what you're talking about."

He plucks a nipple between his teeth.

Show-off.

A beat later, he has me writhing beneath him once again. But just as I think he'll give in and let me have what I want, he flips me over. Hands on my hips, he kneels behind me, sinking in so deep I can barely keep myself upright on my hands and knees.

Holy fuck.

"Dammit, CC. Look at you. Perfect fucking curves, this gorgeous pussy swallowing my cock. A man could get addicted to this."

I can barely breathe, let alone respond. And when his hand slides around my belly and down to my clit, fingers swirling over the bud, I all but face-plant onto the duvet.

He's playing my body like a harp. Strung tight, with every precise pluck of his finger sending me closer and closer to oblivion.

A hand fists my hair, and I cant my ass, wanting him deeper still.

"Quin, please." The raw desperation in my voice should be embarrassing. But he simply leans over, sending kisses up my spine before an arm slips under my rib cage, hauling me up to him. When my back meets his chest, his lips brush my ear. "Keep begging, baby. Every time you make those pretty fucking little noises, I'll give you more."

"I—"

He shakes his head. "No words."

Oh.

He's still. Motionless and waiting.

He wants to hear me. I get nothing, not another inch, until I sing for him.

I send a hand down to my clit before my fingers explore the place we are joined, and we both moan at the same time.

I get one deep, languid thrust.

"Good girl."

Oh god . . .

I lean back, resting my head on his shoulder as I rub my fingertip over my clit. The mewl that follows is dizzying.

"Fuck, that's it." Quin nips my neck, pulling out so slowly it draws more huffy little sounds from my throat. And when he thrusts back in, slower still, I'm all but crying out his name.

"Christ, Celeste. You're my favorite fucking sound."

"More, *please* . . ."

"Sing for me, baby."

He slams into me. This time, he's lodged deep. "I want to see you fall apart when you come all over my cock. We're moving."

"No. Stop, I'm so close," I whine.

He nips the soft flesh of my neck. "We're moving."

Bossy, gorgeous man. He withdraws, leaving me aching for him as he steps off the bed.

"Come here," he growls.

It's all I can do to follow him.

He grabs my hand when I'm off the bed and hauls me into the en suite. My ass meets the cold marble of the vanity a second later. My thighs are pushed wide, hips tugged to the very edge as he sweeps the tip of his cock through my aching entrance.

"Just the tip until you give me those pretty little moans," he says, lodging barely an inch inside me.

My head falls back, hitting the mirror.

Lips close around my nipple.

A finger trails down my belly, stopping short of my clit.

"That's just cruel, Quinnie."

"Just trying on the naughty for size."

"Sweet man, you are no grinch. Sorry to be the one to break it to you, but you're the most incredible man I've ever met."

The words just tumble out, natural and unbridled. And

never a truer word was spoken. Despite the timing, I mean every word.

And his eyes narrow playfully. "You just want the rest of me."

"That's also true, I do. But I meant every word, Quin."

His mouth crashes to mine. I tangle my hands behind his neck, the ache in my core intensifying to something torturous.

He gives me another inch.

And the moan that starts in my chest is captured by him. He takes every sound he elicits from me willingly. Hungrily.

Breaking away from the kiss, I whisper, "Don't make me wait, Quinnie."

He slams into me, and I melt against the marble. Every thrust more punishing than the last, I spiral higher and higher. One hand gripping my hip, his other plays with my clit.

He sweeps his thumb over the sensitive nub, then sends it in circles. Every move he makes has me wrapped up tighter.

Those sounds he was wanting tumble from my mouth consistently.

"Quin," I warn, eyes rolling in my head as my mouth gapes, legs trembling beyond control.

"Fuck, baby, give it to me."

I crash down around him. Bliss explodes through my core as I clamp down, as wave after incredible wave cuts through my body. "Quin, oh my god."

He moans, his thrusts turning sloppy as his forehead hits my chest.

Hot ropes of release follow with a heady, raw growl.

When we've both caught our breath, Quin slides a drawer open and grabs out a washcloth. He runs the water until it's warm. Wetting the rag, he cleans me up with careful, loving strokes of the material. Everything is so sensitive. I shake, holding onto his shoulders as he works.

It's the most intimate, thoughtful gesture I've ever experienced.

"You don't have to . . ." I tug my bottom lip through my teeth.

"Baby, I made a mess of you. The least I can do is clean you up."

I can't help the smile of adoration that blooms.

Scooping me up, he pads for the bed. We crawl between the sheets, and I'm snuggled up against him with my back to his chest before he pulls the blanket over us.

I yawn, and a kiss presses to my temple.

"Just a nap," I mutter, my eyes falling shut.

"Just a few minutes, and we can . . ." He softens against my back, his breathing shallowing out as I fall deeper into that warm, dark, cozy place.

TWENTY-FOUR

QUINTON

I wake up in the wee hours wrapped around Celeste. It's still dark outside.

Good.

A few hours before Maise gets up. A few hours to devour this beautiful woman and have her screaming my name.

Well, maybe not screaming—unless we want to be disturbed ...

I slide my arm from her body. She murmurs but doesn't wake.

Shuffling my way backward under the sheets, I plant myself between her thighs. And *fuck*. Even though I thoroughly destroyed her pussy last night, I am suddenly desperate for it again.

Palming her thighs, I dot kisses around her pretty little clit.

She wriggles, a little moan drifting under the blanket as she starts to look for me. "Quinnie?"

"Yeah, baby."

She moans, her thighs falling open wider.

Hell.

Said it once, I'll say it again. This woman is *fucking perfect*.

"Good morning." I run my tongue through her center.

Her head tilts back on the pillow, hands hunting over the sheet for something to hold. I slide my hands under hers, and she grips tight instantly.

"God, you feel so good," she rasps.

I suckle her clit before lapping at it with my tongue. Her hips roll, chasing the friction my mouth gives.

Greedy little woman this morning.

Good.

I don't plan on being any less needy. Now that we have discovered this thing between us, I don't know if I will ever be able to stop.

Fuck, I don't wanna stop.

With a nip to her sensitive bud, I retract a hand from her hold and slide two fingers inside her.

She bucks against my hand, and the blankets fall away. The first splinter of winter's morning light pierces through the snow-rimmed window. And in the golden glow of the sunrise, Celeste spread wide and bare on my bed is too much. And not fucking enough.

I groan, sweeping through her center before tugging hard on her clit.

"Oh god, Quin," she hums.

But when I clamp down around her and suckle, she sits up, hands tugging at my jaw until I'm looking up at her.

"Move, sweet man."

I'm on my knees a beat later, and her hands are planted on my chest, pushing me back onto my heels. Celeste straddles my lap, wasting no time as she sinks onto me.

The groans that leave both our mouths clash, sending the heady sound around the room. Buried to the hilt with Celeste wrapped around me, my movements are restricted.

She plucks my bottom lip with her teeth before taking up the rhythm between us. And *fuck* . . .

"Good morning, Quinnie."

The lazy smile that grows over her pretty damn face feels like home. *She* feels like home. The very sentiment we shared last night.

"Morning, baby."

Her hands are in my hair as I drop my mouth to her peaks. Her pussy strangles my cock even harder as I lick, suckle, and bite her closer to ecstasy, one peak after the other.

"Fuck. We're starting every day this way. That's my new Christmas wish."

"You only get one, mister, and you already used it," she coos.

"Says who," I growl.

"Me. But since we're negotiating, I guess another one won't hurt."

"If this is how you negotiate, Celeste, I'm fucked."

"It appears so," she says with a giggle, her chest bouncing in my damn face. *Torturous little woman.*

Her dark hair falls over her shoulders and curtains her breasts as she leans forward and claims my mouth.

I pry her open, my tongue taking over every inch of her. She rises and falls so slowly, eliciting a heady groan.

As she breaks from my kiss, head falling back, I seize a hard peak between my teeth and bite down. She jerks, and it's like fucking heaven.

"Ah, god." Rolling her hips, her breath stalls out.

"You like a little pain?" I grind out around her nipple.

A sweet moan slips out before she utters, "I like everything you do to me, Quin."

Christ.

The caveman in me rises to the surface quicker than I can restrain it. And when she slides a hand behind herself and traces a fingertip over my balls, my restraint snaps altogether. I slap her ass, hard.

She rocks into me with a harsh gasp.

"My turn," I growl, manhandling her as I rise and move from the bed, crossing the room until she's perched on the low windowsill. Slamming her into the cold glass, I spread her thighs wider still, gripping her hips with one hand and curling my fingers around her neck with the other.

Pulling out slowly, I snap out, "Watch."

Her gaze drops to the place we are connected. Where my hard length penetrates her soft, wet cunt.

It takes my fucking breath away.

"We fit so damn perfect, Celeste."

I rock into her, sending a hand to tease that little nub of hers that has her all worked up. A strangled whimper leaves her throat.

She arches off the glass.

My hand slides from her neck to one breast in a punishing grip, flicking the nipple with my thumb. My nail scrapes the tender peak with every pass.

She grips the side of the window frame.

I pick up the pace, but the glass groans with the force. With a growl, I tug her onto my waist and pad from the window.

"Where are we going?" she breathes.

The fireplace is all but out. I kneel on the floor and grab the poker, sending embers into the chimney. I toss on another two logs as she kisses and nips my neck, my jaw.

"Hurry up, sweet man. I can't wait. I don't care if we're cold."

"I care if you're cold, baby."

Plus, I intend on fucking her on every surface and fulfilling her Christmas wish. Even if it takes weeks.

Fuck, I hope it takes years.

When I have reasonable flames leaping from the hard-wood logs and kindling, she's all but frantic. Suckling, touching. Hips wiggling in protest of the intermission.

"You're an impatient little thing, baby."

"You not moving is torture," she whines.

I chuckle, and she narrows her eyes as she wriggles her hips.

"You want everything I got?"

"Everything. As much as you'll give me."

Everything may tak—

She rises on her knees now, leaving me reeling in the wake of her fluttering pussy. When I slip from her wet entrance altogether, it's too much.

"No," I growl, grabbing her arm before she can rise to her feet.

Where the hell does she think she's going?

But when she turns back, a wry smile on her lips, I realize I've been played.

"Fucking brat."

She simply sinks to her knees, giving me her back. When she sweeps her dark hair over one shoulder to expose her spine and cants her ass, I can't—

"Fuck me, Quinnie. I'm not playing anymore," she rasps.

Hands snatching hips, I push her face into the rug as I nudge her knees wider. She turns back, that bottom lip tugging inward between her teeth. I tease her entrance with the tip of my cock.

She wants this badly, so I'll make her wait.

Slick need coats her thighs, and I almost give in to her desperate little whimper. *Almost.*

But as the room gets brighter by the minute, I realize our window is closing faster than I would like. I slam into her. She cries out, legs spreading wider, ass canting up further as if she needs me deeper.

I pull out and slam into her again.

Her hand reaches back, hunting . . .

I bundle her hair in my fist and tug her head back. She rises halfway up, suspended midway by my hold on her hair and held down by the angle she's using to push back onto my cock with every lazy stroke I give her.

The fire warms us. Sweat trickles down my spine as I power into her.

Her body trembles as it takes mine. The soft, tight walls of her pussy flutter, and I send my fingers to find her clit.

"Come on, baby, keep granting my Christmas wishes. Come all over my cock. Strangle the fuck out of it."

"Quin. Oh my god." She rises a little further, the angle changing enough to elicit sparks of electricity through my core and along my limbs.

My pace quickens as I swirl my thumb around her nub, sending her shaking against my body. She's barely breathing.

I thrust up into her hard, intensifying the depth and pace. She falls against my chest, bucking as she clamps down around my cock in vicious, beautiful waves.

I loose my hold on her hair and grip a breast, pinching the nipple as I press wet, open-mouthed kisses just below her ear. "Fuck, CC, a man could die from this much . . ."

Her waves double down, my knees nearly buckling.

A low growl leaves my chest as my release chases hers. And when I shoot ropey lengths of seed into her, I bite down on her shoulder to muffle the moan that would wake up the entire house.

A breath later, fine hands weave into my hair, turning my head until my mouth is pressed to hers. Still inside her, I kiss her like it's the first time we've touched.

And when she puts just a little space between us, her big brown doe eyes meet mine and she whispers, "Best Christmas wish ever, sweet man."

Our clothes are barely on when the door rattles. Fuck, that's right—I locked it last night. Good thing, since Maise apparently woke up with the damn birds.

I wait until CC is dressed and snuggled up in my bed before padding to the door to open it.

"Daddy, I heard CC." Hand on her hips, she scans the space behind me until her eyes land on Celeste in my bed. "Hey! You had a sleepover without me?"

She pushes past me, flying into the bed and curling up next to CC.

"Morning, sweetheart," CC says, dotting a kiss to her hair.

Maise rolls to face her. "How come you didn't invite me?"

"Oh, well." Celeste glances at me then returns her gaze to Maise. "I was kind of scared in my house all by myself, and your daddy said I could sleep here. Sorry, Maise. You were already sound asleep, and I didn't want to wake you."

"Alright, that's okay." Maise tucks her hands under her head. "But next time, I'm coming."

I pad to CC's side of the bed and lead down, kissing her cheek. "I'll make the coffee."

Her hand catches my wrist as I go to leave. "Just five more minutes?"

She wants to snuggle . . . All three of us?

Maise laughs. "Lady, you have it bad."

I try and fail to tamp down a chuckle as Celeste tickles Maise.

"I'll have you know, your daddy is one of my favorite people."

I swallow past the growing stone in my throat.

"And me too?" Maise asks.

"You too, my sweet."

I leave the two gigglepots in the warmth of my bed and head downstairs to fetch the coffee. When I make it back upstairs with a tray of caffeine and various breakfast foods, they are sitting up on the bed, braiding hair.

"Oh! I need clips!" Maise rushes from the bed and from the room as I set the tray on the bedside.

"I think that went okay?" Celeste gives me a cringy

smile, like she's not sure how to act after almost being busted by my daughter.

"She'll get used to you being here. Maybe she'll even knock next time."

I sink onto the side of the bed.

"You think so?" CC's face brightens.

"She's already got a vision board with you on it, baby. You did that."

"Oh, really. Like we're BFFs or something?" She smiles.

A choked sound catches in my throat. "More like a . . . mother."

TWENTY-FIVE

CELESTE

"Oh." The instant the sound passes my lips, I know it's the wrong reaction.

It's not the one I would go with if I had time to think about the sentiment. I've just . . .

His hand tilts my head, forcing my gaze to his. "No one expects that of you—well, besides Maise. But this is whatever you want it to be, Celeste. Whatever we want it to be, but if it's just a temporary thing, we'll keep it on the down-low, okay?"

Um. Okay . . . ?

Do I want to sneak around with this man or be his baby mama? What kind of choice is that?

"I think I should go," I whisper.

"No, CC." Hurt and panic flood his gaze. "God, can we just rewind like five minutes?"

"It's fine. I have to get ready for Dad's arrival today, anyway."

"No, please stay." He's hauling me into his hold. "Fuck, that didn't come out right."

"I would, but . . . I-I can't."

Extracting myself from his tense embrace, I'm off the bed and out of his bedroom a heartbeat later.

"Tell Maise I'll see her later," I mutter before flying down the stairs.

I'm out the front door and across the snowy ground before my brain catches up with my actions.

And fuck.

I flaked. I did it again. My stupid insecurities screwing me over—again.

The man just doesn't want his daughter to get hurt. A reasonable request. And shit, I'm sure I'd do the same if I was in his shoes. If I was a parent.

The thought sends a streak of panic through me. I can't even take care of one grown man I've known my entire life. What kind of parent would I make?

The second the front door to my house clicks shut, I slump against it, head back and eyes closed. "Shit, Celeste."

My pocket vibrates with my alarm, and I shake off the last ten minutes, forcing it to the back of my mind. I need to focus on Dad now. That's all today is for. Getting him home and settled. Hopefully the medications have kicked in by now and he's feeling more like his old self.

If I could be granted one last Christmas wish . . . it would be that my dad was home and happy.

His quality of life as good as he deserves.

I start with coffee. Every dutiful daughter needs a little spark at the beginning of their day. After I make up his bed with clean sheets, I fix the sunroom to make sure it's just as he will be expecting. His chair, blanket, and of course, Mark Twain.

When the clock ticks over to ten a.m., I grab my bag and phone and head for the truck.

A few minutes later, I'm pulling into the hospital parking lot. And when I make it inside, the place is quiet. I ask for Dad at the reception desk and barely a minute passes when his doctor appears.

"Celeste, how are you?"

He's not really asking, but I say, "Good. How's Dad?"

He tilts his head to one side, indicating for me to come with him. I push to my feet and follow as he takes us back to the small room we were in last time.

As the door shuts, he waves toward a chair. "Have a seat. I want to talk to you about the medications before you decide to take him home."

"Okay." I sit, my ass barely in the chair as I clutch my bag in my lap.

"So, our initial change of meds didn't work as we expected. In fact, he became more agitated not even twenty-four hours later. With that, we made another change and added something to calm him down. This was effective, but—"

"Like a sedative?"

"Yes, exactly."

My brows fall. We never talked about sedating him. And the thought of him living in a daze doesn't sit right with me.

"At this point, he can go home if you have help moving him around and he remains on the first floor of your home. Stairs won't be safe."

"Can't you reduce the dose of the sedative?"

He sighs. "We worked in increments to ensure we had a balance of safety and effectiveness. But Celeste, I have to say, we recommend he is placed into care as soon as possible. The sedatives cannot be used long-term. As I'm sure you will understand why."

"So the plan has always been to take him from his home. This is what you're saying?" Pain lances through my chest, so tight I can barely breathe.

"We believe at this stage of his disease, it is his best option."

He gives me an empathetic smile.

No.

The weight of a thousand tiny mistakes I've made my entire life crashes down on me. My hands shake, my body numbing further with every shallow breath.

"I-I have to talk to my brother and sister," I utter, rising on shaky legs.

I came home for one thing, and I couldn't even do that. I couldn't take care of my father. I can hardly look after myself. Who was I kidding . . .

I push from the door, leaving the doctor mid-sentence.

Tears burn and my throat closes over. But I slide my phone from my bag and dial my sister.

She picks up on the second ring. "Hey, CC. What's happening?"

I sniff, trying to haul in a lungful of air. "Nothing good. The doctor says Dad has to go into a home."

"Oh, that wasn't the plan. It's too early yet."

"He's deteriorated," I say softly.

"Did you stick to the routine and menu Marie left? It was crucial to slowing down the progress of the disease."

I hate it when she talks down to me, but right now . . . I deserve it.

"I tried, as much as possible. Mostly, I did, yes."

"Mostly." Her tone sinks, along with my gut.

And when a tired sigh comes through the phone, my chin wobbles. "I really did try. I thought he was doing okay, you know."

I'm sobbing into the phone now, which will only annoy my sister further. She hates criers.

"Listen to me. Just do as the doctors ask, okay? You tried your best. What matters now is Dad gets the best care he can."

"Sure, right. Okay."

I suck back a sob.

"And Celeste," she adds. "Merry Christmas."

The line goes dead.

Merry Christmas to you, too.

Not brave enough to fill my brother in, I leave that task to my sister. Instead, I turn back and push through the door to the small appointment room.

The doctor is tapping away on his tablet but looks up when I sit back down. "How do I apply for a place for Dad?"

"There's a few forms to fill out, finances to sort, etc. I've already emailed it to you as per your sister's request."

My mouth falls open. She already knew. She already knew and didn't think to include me in the decision, let alone the discussion that I'm guessing happened over the last few days.

While I was . . .

"You know what, I just want to see Dad, if you don't mind." I rise, and he follows.

"Sure, I'll show you the way."

We walk down the hallway until we come to a communal dayroom of sorts. Elderly people sit around in various conditions, all in recliner lounges. Some doing activities and some asleep. I spot Dad right away. He's reading in the chair by an old piano topped with Christmas decorations.

It's only now that I let my gaze wander and take in the festively decorated space.

It's . . . lovely.

I cross the floor to where Dad sits. His head is tilted to one side, and I doubt he's even read a word. His eyes are mostly glazed over.

"Is he sedated now?" I turn back and ask the doctor.

"A little, yes."

"If he stays, can he be weaned off them?"

"Mostly, when he settles in."

My heart twists in my chest at the sight of him like this. Doped out and only half there.

"Once the paperwork and finances are sorted, how long until he gets a place?"

The doctor taps his tablet, scrolling for a while before he looks back up. "There's a place over in the medium-care facility if we're quick."

"Then be quick. Email my sister back, she can have it all taken care of. After all, I'm just the help." I turn my back to him and sit on the arm of Dad's chair. He looks up, as if in slow motion.

"Hey Daddy," I whisper. Too emotional to worry about which name is best for this situation. I just want him to be my dad. Not Hank or Mr. Black. Just Daddy.

"Hey, honey. What are you doing here?"

I huff a sad laugh. He's still there, despite all the drugs they have given him.

"Just here to see you." I dot a kiss to his forehead.

He pats my cheek and returns to his book. "Have you read this one? It's incredible, Tisha."

Loosing a strained sigh, I nod. "Yeah, it is."

We chat about the book in his hands, even though I've never read a word of it. His words slur when he tires from my visit. So I just sit with him. He listens as I hold his hand, running through every wonderful memory we've ever shared, letting my memory do the work for us this time.

And the contentment and happiness that shine through the eyes that have always seen me with all the love a parent can give fill my own with tears. If this is the last time we get to have this, it's a moment I will treasure for the rest of my days.

A tap to my shoulder disturbs me twenty minutes later.

"Visiting hours are over, lovely." The same nurse I met last time gives me a genuine smile, and I stand.

"Bye, Daddy. See you another day, okay?"

He smiles up at me, but I can tell by the vacant look in his eyes he doesn't remember. The moment is over for him.

Sandy slides her arm through mine. "It will get better, I promise."

I can't even look at her, having to scrunch my face to stem the tears that won't let up.

When we're out of the communal space, she stops in the hallway and hauls me into a hug. Her hand rubs circles on my back. "Every time you think you've not done enough, I want you to remember all the times your family was happy. That's all you can take from this disease." She holds me at arm's length. "Alright?"

I nod. "Okay."

"Oh, sweetheart, he's in good hands here."

"I hope so."

She swats my arm, and I chuckle a strained, awkward sound.

"I know he will be, I will make sure of it. Now, you get home and focus on getting ready for your Christmas. Don't let this steal your holiday joy, hon. Don't give it that kind of power."

It's all I can do to stare at her.

After Mom's death, that's all my family ever did. Let tragedy eat away at everything good left behind. Us. We were the ones left behind, and the holidays were not the only thing we lost when we lost mom. We fractured as a family. Three siblings drifted apart, with no central pull back home. Or maybe the hurt kept us away. Coming home was—is—too painful.

But I've walked through it now.

That phase of my life ends now.

Sandy stands in my space, studying me. "You good?"

"Yeah, I think so, for the first time in a long time. Thank you."

She tilts her head, emotion twisting her face. "Merry Christmas, Celeste."

"Merry Christmas, Sandy."

She waves me off, and I walk back outside to the truck with a renewed spark. It only took losing the one last anchor I had to this life to realize I wasn't really living.

And for a moment, I'm envious of Dad. He's no longer

tethered to the sorrow that consumed us for decades. He found a way out.

A way free.

I'll be damned if I don't do the same.

TWENTY-SIX

QUINTON

The letter in my hand crinkles beneath my fist. I've read it three times, and the words on the page refuse to change.

A letter of custody settlement.

My worst fear coming to a head. Maisey being taken away from me.

But the letter in my hand reads loud and clear—*Stella Joan Ramsey hereby applies for full custody of Maisey Emmaline MacKelvie (age 5).*

Fucking hell.

Only two days before Christmas. She has to be fucking kidding me, right?

That's a low blow, even for her. I take note of the letterhead, a family legal firm from Boston.

So, she's back. Just our damn luck.

Over my rotting corpse is she waltzing back into our lives. She should have stayed away.

"Daddy, you're going to get a wrinkle face like Mr. Black." Maise spoons cereal into her mouth. The milk dribbles down her chin, but she catches it with a hand and leans over the bowl, chewing ferociously. "Wos wong?"

"Don't talk with your mouth full, kiddo. And nothing."

"Why do you look all angry and stuff?"

She tilts her head. Perceptive little girl. I fold the letter and return it to its envelope. "I'm not angry, Maise. Just annoyed."

"At that letter?" She points with her spoon, dripping milk over the table.

"Maybe. Forget it, hey. Go and get ready for the sleigh ride, might be a line."

In this tiny town, probably not. But anything to get her moving. She throws another spoonful in her mouth before rushing from the table. Any other day I'd make her eat more, but my head has been thoroughly messed up by one piece of paper.

Clearing the table, I slip the letter into the back pocket of my jeans. When our coats are on and Maise is bundled up in a scarf and beanie, we leave the house. The truck rattles to life in the cold weather, and I let her run for a beat to warm up the engine.

"Can I go over to see Celeste when we get home? I need some BFF time. No offense, Daddy." She pins me with a serious look, like I'll say no if I take her at any less than her word.

"Sure, kiddo. Maybe we'll see her at the sleigh ride."

Maise pulls her belt on, and I reverse the truck onto the street. The snow-lined town with its two sets of traffic lights only has us driving for around five minutes before I turn the old girl into Maple Acres Farm.

Caleb's family has been stupid busy with the holidays, between folks rolling in everyday to come pick out their perfect tree at the Christmas tree farm and the reindeer that now stand along the white wooden fence on the edge of the field.

I pull in by the big barn that also serves as a makeshift tree collecting spot. Maise is out of her booster seat a second later, the back door opening as she jumps down. Folks are rolling in, and many are already lining up inside the roped-off area up by the main farmhouse.

"Come on, Daddy, look how big the line is already!"

I'm dragged along until we join said line. Maise pouting as she discovers some of her school friends up ahead. But my head is anywhere but here.

Every worst-case scenario that could come to light with the letter burning a hole in my back pocket has me on edge and in my head. What the hell is Stella thinking?

She hasn't seen Maise since the week she was born.

How the hell does she think this is going to work?

A soft hand slips into mine. But Maise is a few paces up, talking to someone she must know from school.

"Hey, Quinnie."

Celeste's cinnamon and floral shrouds me as she leans into my side.

"Hey."

I glance at her, but I'm still lost to worry. Her hand squeezes mine, and it's then I realize Hank is not with her. She came alone.

"Where's Hank?" I ask, and the second the words leave my mouth her face falls. "Baby, what happened? Why didn't you text me? Or come over?"

"He's okay. But he's . . ." She glances up the line, her gaze finding Maise before she reconnects with mine. "He's not coming home." Her chin wobbles.

"Ah fuck, Celeste. I'm so sorry." I haul her into my arms, and she melts into my hold.

"I thought we had more time," she says softly.

You and me both, baby.

She unravels from my hold in time to catch a rushing kid donning a beanie and rainbow scarf. She lifts Maise up, planting her on her hip. "Hey, sweetheart."

"CC, you have to ride with us! Daddy, CC has to ride with us."

"Sure, kiddo."

I watch them together as Maise snuggles into Celeste and they chatter away about the farm and the reindeer.

It isn't long before we hear sleigh bells and the clip-clop of hooves over the cold, hard ground. The entire crowd turns in one motion, the gasps and oohs and aahs echoing down the line. Maise squeals with delight, and CC chuckles at her, the smile so wide on her beautiful face, joy radiating from them both. And to an outsider, they would look like mother and daughter.

And that burns.

So damn bittersweet. Because if things go sideways, neither of my favorite girls will ever have the chance to have that together.

We wait for way too long as each group has a twenty-minute ride. The six reindeer, harnessed in red leather gear, elegantly walk on after collecting each new lot of passengers before breaking into a lope with Caleb at the reins.

Finally, we reach the front of the line.

Maise is almost beside herself when the sleigh slows in front of us and the folks disembark.

CC puts her down, and Maise slides her little hand into Celeste's before lacing her fingers with mine. The three of us stay joined as Maise climbs the silver drop-down stairs and into the white-and-gold sleigh. Letting Maise go, I help CC up before jumping in beside the girls.

"Ready?" Caleb turns back with a shit-eating grin.

I glance at Maise.

She sits up, clearing her throat before saying eloquently, "Ready, sir."

Caleb chuckles and slaps the reins. "Walk on."

Celeste's smile is fixed. She watches with wonder as Maise takes in the sleigh as the six reindeer pull us along at a steady pace, rounding the farmhouse along a snowy path until it opens up into a hilly field. The glistening white rolling spans sends crisp air around us as we slip along its surface.

"Hup hup," Caleb calls, slapping the reins twice, and the deer burst into a lope. The sleigh lurches forward a little before settling into a quick pace.

Maisey's grip tightens around my fingers, and I lean down. "You good, kiddo?"

"Perfect, Daddy. This is so perfect."

"It's pretty good."

She rolls her eyes at me but leans into my side. I wrap my arm around her small shoulders.

How can I lose my baby girl?

It wouldn't just devastate me, it would do much worse to her.

Stella has one hell of a fight on her hands if she thinks she's going to get what she wants.

Celeste leans over. "This is amazing."

We fly over a rise and shoot down the other side. It's pretty fucking awesome. But the best part is the two girls I'm sharing it with.

And there is no way in hell I'm losing this.

"We'll be fine." Celeste cups my face. "I've got this. Go sort that crazy, selfish woman out. And come home to us for Christmas."

Every inch of my being rejects the fact that I have to be away from CC and Maise for two nights as I haul her in close. "Thought you hated Christmas, baby."

She pushes back, meeting my gaze. "It's growing on me."

I give her a lazy smile, dotting a kiss to her lips. "Good. You deserve a little tinsel in your life."

She rolls her eyes at me. I swear she got that from Maise. Who I'm leaving with Celeste. Or I'm leaving Celeste with Maise? At any rate, they will be here, in my house, together. Until I come back from Boston, hopefully with this custody bullshit sorted.

"I'll miss you both something fierce. Make sure you stoke the fires, and if you need anything, call me. If I'm not answering, try Caleb."

It pains me to have a backup. But I won't leave them alone with nobody to call. My ego isn't that ridiculous.

"We will be fine, Quinnie. Go, get your baby sorted."

Fuck. I want to. But I can't get my feet to move. My hold on Celeste tightens. And what I wouldn't give to have her by my side through this.

That thought grows roots, unfurling into something huge and permanent. I swallow past the stone growing in my throat. And now I need to leave before I do something stupid, like propose.

Damn, my head is all over the place.

"Bye, baby."

Maise wanders into the foyer, pulling her holiday sweater over her head. "Daddy, can I have candy while you're gone?"

I squat down and she falls into my lap. "You'll have to ask CC. And bedtime is still seven-thirty, eat all your veggies, and no more than an hour of screen time, kiddo."

She sags in my grip. "Oh, alright . . ."

I chuckle. "I'll miss you, Maise."

It's the first time we've ever been apart, and I hope she will be okay. But I have faith that her and CC will be just fine without me. For a few days . . . It's only a few days.

"Bye, Daddy. I love you."

Emotion clogs my throat, but I manage to say, "Love you, too, kiddo." I press a kiss to her forehead.

I let her go and guide her into CC's space. Celeste slides her arms over Maise's shoulders and leans down, hugging her tight.

I walk out and close the door before my heart craps out.

Caleb waits in his truck, idling on the side of the curb. I toss my bag in the back and climb into the front passenger seat.

"All set, bud?" he asks, pulling the truck onto the street.

I can't drag my gaze from my house, the girls standing by the window huddled together.

"Yeah, let's get this over with."

TWENTY-SEVEN

CELESTE

Maise dances around the tree as I wrap gifts for Quin and my dad on her living room floor. The music that used to instill sadness and overwhelm in me sends her prancing around the sofa as she spins and waves her hands around to "It's Beginning to Look a Lot Like Christmas".

Michael Bublé edition, if I've got the swoony tone pinned down.

The fire crackles, sending its warm and flickering glow around the softly lit room. It is a little surreal being here without Quinton, yet the house feels like more of a home than next door with Dad gone.

The thought of him surrounded by strangers makes my chest squeeze. But I understand that to him, everyone is a stranger now.

I tie off the red ribbon on his gift, another classic book I picked up from the Christmas market before the tree lighting a week ago.

Wow, that was only a week ago? It feels like years' worth of stuff has happened in the last seven days. In the last month, if I'm honest.

"CC, can you run me a bubble bath?"

Maise flops onto the sofa, and I spin on my seat and look up at her. "All out of moves, little lady?"

"Dancing is exhausting." Her head lolls to one side.

Pushing to my feet, I scoop her up and onto my hip. "Come on then, let's get you washed and ready for bed."

When we walk from the living room toward the stairs, she twists in my hold. "Daddy would never let me stay up this late."

I glance at the old clock on the mantel that shows ten past nine.

Shit, so much for her bedtime. The night just got away from us, with dinner, dancing, present wrapping, and a whole ton of laughter and fun.

Something warm and permanent fills me to the bone. *Happiness.*

"I won't tell if you don't," I say, tapping her little button nose.

She uses a hand to zip her lips, locking it and stuffing the hand in her pocket before shaking her head.

I chuckle. "Our little secret, hey, sweetheart."

She snuggles into me, small arms sliding around my neck as I ascend the stairs. With a quick bath and towel-down, she's ready for bed. I tuck her in snug as a bug in a rug style, just like Quin does.

As I go to leave, she slips one arm from her confines and grabs my wrist. "CC?"

I turn back. "Yeah, baby?"

"Stay."

Stay?

"Okay, just for a little while." I sit on the edge of her bed, but she pats the pillow. I lay down and she wiggles closer, her small hand slipping into mine.

"I miss Daddy," she whispers, her face falling from joy to sadness in a heartbeat.

I give her hand a squeeze and roll over, hugging her into my chest. Running my hand over her head, I sigh. "Me too, sweetheart."

She sniffles, and it's now I feel her little body shake with a sob.

"This is the first time you and Daddy have been apart?" I ask.

She nods against my chest.

"That's tough, kiddo."

Especially since it's always been her and Quin against the world. She doesn't know an existence without him around.

"You know what, a long time ago, I felt a little like you are now."

"Your daddy was gone, too?" she asks, her big brown eyes, now soaked with tears, drifting up.

"My mom was. And I was so sad. But you know what?"

"What," she utters, her hands close around my own as I brush a damp strand from her face.

"Snuggles always helped."

I cuddle her against me tight, tickling her ribs until she is giggling and wriggling, making a mess of her blankets.

I give her a reprieve, pushing up on one elbow as I roll toward her. "You're not alone, Maise. I'm right here. You need me, just say so, okay?"

"You promise?" Maise settles down again, cuddling into me.

"I promise," I say, kissing the top of her head.

"Always?" she whispers.

The last breath catches in my throat.

Always . . . in this life where we have so little control over so many things.

But those are grown-up thoughts and worries.

"Always." I rub her cheek with my thumb, studying her pretty brown eyes as I give her a warm smile.

That's all she needs right now. Someone who loves her.

How many times have I been that little girl, over and over in my life, despite getting older every year?

And without that steady constant, you can find yourself floundering like I was for over a decade. Not this time. Not *this* little girl. I hug her closer and sink onto the pillow. "Get some rest, sweetie. One more sleep to go."

"One more sleep and Daddy's home . . ." Maise yawns, her eyes fluttering closed.

When her breathing settles, I brush her hair from her face and extricate myself from the tangle of covers and limbs. Pulling the door closed, I pad to Quin's room.

The second I open the door, his sandalwood and spice hits me . . .

Maise isn't the only one who misses Daddy.

I scoff at the thought, but the amusement fades as I realize I do. I do miss him. Things feel off-balance without him. Not grounded and certain, just anxiously floating somewhere up near the ceiling, like a hot burst of a summer afternoon squall.

I ready for bed and crawl beneath the covers. But this time, I make a point of sleeping on Quin's side. With Dad in the home and Maise in her own bed, the reminder of Quin is all that I can grab onto.

I hope he's making progress with Maisey's mom. God, I can't imagine how life would be without Maise in it. Quin must be beside himself. I know I would be.

Losing Dad to his disease, even though he is only miles away, was hard enough. And he's my parent, not my child.

Suddenly, the thought of life without Maise—without Quin is too small. My chest caves in on itself, and a weight I can't explain settles in the space.

Would Quin leave if he lost Maisey? He only moved here to give her a better childhood. This house would still be his, but would he want to stay if it was just him rattling around in it?

God, I should have gone with him.

Maybe I could have helped?

The door creaks open, and a small figure pads to the other side of the bed and slides in. Before I can take stock, I'm reaching for her, pulling her close and wrapping the blanket around the both of us.

"CC?" she says, her little voice so small and wobbly.

"Yeah, baby?"

"I love you."

"I love you, too, Maise."

Her fingers curl around the opening of my pajama shirt.

Love you, too, sweet girl.

And I miss your daddy more than I thought I could ever miss another human being.

TWENTY-EIGHT

QUINTON

"You've got to be shitting me." I grind my molars like they're responsible for the clusterfuck in front of me right now.

"Language, Quinton." Stella frowns, sending a hand over her two-piece skirt suit that's far too short to be appropriate. "See, red flag right there. What kind of parent uses that kind of profanity regularly?"

"You want to talk about red flags? Woman, you're a goddamn walking red flag."

My grip tightens on the too-small glass of water that we were offered when we sat down in this over-done, rip-off excuse of a family law conference room.

I sit with my representation on one side of the long, polished mahogany table. Turns out having a lawyer on call came in handy, especially during the holidays. Stella and some guy that looks like she plucked him right out of *Grease* sit on the other side.

"My client has evidence that you have withheld your daughter from her. And on these grounds, we are filing for full custody." Grease Danny says, thumbing a stain on his double-breasted jacket.

Kendall, our family lawyer for decades now, his age showing with his snowy -white hair and weathered face, leans forward. "Do you have a signed affidavit?"

Stella slides a small stack of papers over the table, giving me a smirk that could haunt the devil.

Kendall plucks it up, flipping through the pages and stopping to read some parts. He hums a sound of disapproval before dropping the document to the table. "Insubstantial."

"Mr. MacKelvie moved the child without consulting my client. He failed to forward an address after they had moved. My client has spent the last five years without her daughter. We will be proceeding with this matter."

The hell she did.

I go to open my mouth, and Kendall pats my hand like the old man he is, shaking his head softly.

"We in the family court are not interested in the welfare of parents, Mr. Smythe. We are in the business of doing what is best for the child. Period."

"How do you know I'm not the best parent for her? I've never had the chance. It's my turn. I want her." Stella pouts.

Kendall leans forward and holds Stella's gaze that's now

burning with fury. "Let me let you in on a little secret, Miss Ramsey—good parents don't walk away from their child after the first seven days of their life. Good parents don't put their career and life before their child. And good parents most certainly do not try to rip their child from the only safe place they've ever known." Kendall stands. "We're done here."

I follow his lead and stand, walking from the room.

Screaming starts the second the heavy glass door closes behind us. I turn back to see Stella throwing her arms around at Grease Danny. Smythe, was it? He's placating her, running his hand through his gelled hair.

And with this little display, there is no way in hell's handbasket that woman is getting near Maise, ever.

"So, we're all done here?" I ask Kendall as we walk through the foyer of the Smythe and Sanders office.

"Unfortunately, I've seen these types of things too many times to give you the answer you want. It's more likely she will proceed, if she has the funding. However, a court will not remove a child from a parent without due cause."

"What does that mean?"

He frowns. "Things like neglect, poverty, and access. Which she has not had."

"So, there is a chance she could win . . . but"—I spin and point to the building now behind us—"you just said—"

He holds up a hand. "I doubt she could win this. But there is always a chance. It would be remiss of me to tell you this is a cakewalk, Quinton. It may not be. Time will tell."

"So, we've solved nothing."

"We've done our recon." He slaps my arm. "Try not to worry about it, son. Enjoy your Christmas. She may go home and realize it's too much trouble."

"Yeah, right." I swallow past the stone that's grown in my throat. "Merry Christmas, Kendall."

He tips his old man flat cap and smiles at me before walking down the snowy Boston street.

Merry *fucking* Christmas . . .

The doors behind me slide open and heels clack toward me.

I brace for the onslaught as the ferocious blonde I once thought was the love of my life stalks toward me, her face tugged into a snarl.

I could almost laugh at how ridiculous she looks, if I wasn't here trying to keep my family safe.

"You won't win this, Quinton. Judges don't keep mothers from their babies. Not everyone's a barbarian like you." She shoulder-slams me, not even getting me to budge, as she marches past.

She winces as she walks away. It's all I can do to shake my head at her.

Geez.

When she disappears into the crowd of city folk rushing around the last day before Christmas, the only thing I want to do is get home to my girls.

Like, now.

'Twas the night before Christmas and all through the house . . . two impatient girls pace, waiting on one man. And he isn't Santa Claus. The weather has settled in, making travel from Boston to Grafton slow and a little tricky.

We've had one sketchy phone call from Quin and a few text updates on his location in the last half of the day.

Now every minute feels like an hour.

"He's going to be here soon, honey. I'm sure."

Maise pouts as she paces. "Hurry up, Daddy. How can he miss Christmas?"

Her little huff makes me laugh.

I grab her and tickle the pout from her face. "He'll be here soon, kiddo. Let's make some hot cocoa to pass the time."

"Fine." She rolls her eyes, head tilting upward to the ceiling.

The house is cleaned from top to bottom. Apparently Maise and I both clean when we're anxious. The tree glitters under the strings of lights and the fire crackles away, thanks to instructions from Maise after I forgot everything Quinton told me before he left.

We pad to the kitchen, and I pull out two mugs. My hand hovers for a third, but I don't want to get her hopes up. I leave it there and put the kettle on.

Maise sinks onto a counter stool, planting her chin in her hands. "What if he doesn't get back in time?"

"He will. Have a little faith."

I give her my best smile, but her expression doesn't change. *Yeah, I don't believe me, either.*

The last time we waited for someone to come home on Christmas Eve, she didn't. The gut-churning feeling that follows the dark memory burns something fierce behind my eyes.

Nope.

That is not what's happening here.

"CC?"

"Yeah, baby?" I turn from the blank spot on the wall that has snagged my gaze.

"The kettle's boiling."

The squeal fades in and I shake the morbid thought and very real worry away, heading for the kettle.

"Right. Cocoa time."

"Is that what happened to your mommy?"

How the . . .

"She was coming home from a Christmas decoration making class she was running and—"

Maise gasps.

Shit. God, Celeste, really?

I round the counter and hug her close. "That's not what is happening here, okay? Your dad is a capable, brave man. And he has a really, really good reason to make it home."

She looks up, the fear not abated from her face. "Christmas isn't until tomorrow."

I chuckle, but it's strained, as a tear sails down my cheek. "No, kiddo. You. You're his reason."

She studies my face for a beat before adding, "And you, too. He has *two* reasons now."

Tears are pouring down my stupid face and I scrunch it up, trying to stem the flow. It doesn't help, so I cuddle Maise close. When we've both recovered, I pour the cocoa and we decide to watch a Christmas movie on the flat-screen that barely gets used in the living room.

"Oh, I forgot something," I say, jumping up and walking to the foyer. Grabbing the basket I brought over, I leave it covered up, returning to the sofa and plopping onto the cushions. "It's a little late, but since we are sentries at our Christmas post, we could use a treat." I hand her a candy apple.

Her brown eyes light up, wide with joy. "Daddy will be mad I'm having candy so late . . ."

She unwraps the paper from the apple regardless. I open one for myself and take a bite. It's sweet, tangy, and so juicy. The crisp crunch of the apple is euphoric.

Red candy sticks to Maisey's lips, and she licks them as she devours the apple. Delight wraps her features. And I take note of the small moment of happiness after hours of waiting and worrying.

We settle in. The animated Christmas movie takes over, the long day finally taking its toll as we relax into the soft sofa cushions. Just around the midpoint of the movie, Maise slumps against me, her eyes closed.

"Night, sweet girl."

I watch the rest of the movie and another starts. I glance at the clock.

11:15 p.m.

Come on, Quinnie.

A cityscape under a snow blanket decorated with too much Christmas flair bursts onto the screen. I let my eyes fall shut . . . just for a moment.

The sofa bobs and rocks. Something thuds rhythmically below me. I jerk awake.

"Hey, you're okay, baby." Warm lips press to

my forehead. Arms cradle me to a wall of chest. Then, blue eyes shine down at me.

"Quinnie, you're home?" I breathe.

"Yeah, baby. I'm home."

"I was so worried." My voice breaks.

The staircase disappears and he rounds the banister, heading for his room. "Sorry it took me so long."

My hands gravitate to his jaw. He dips his head, his mouth on mine. Breaking away, he rumbles, "Mmmm, candy."

I giggle. Red candy is smudged on his mouth. Which means it must be . . .

"Oh shit. Is it all over my face?"

He chuckles. "Just a little."

I gasp, lifting up out of his arms a little way with a start. "Maise."

"She's already in bed. And her face looks worse than yours." He nips at my lips, my chin, and my cheek.

God, how much candy did I get on my face?

"Put me down. I need to wash up."

"Nope." He walks into his bedroom, bypassing the bed and heading straight to the en suite. "I've been waiting hours to devour this beautiful body of yours."

"You have?" I utter.

"Yeah." He puts me down on my feet and turns on the shower. Deft fingers have my pajama top on the floor a moment later. "And I'm done waiting."

He sinks to one knee and slides my pajama bottoms over

my hips and to the floor. My panties disappear next. "Get wet with me, Celeste."

His flannel shirt falls away, and he's tugging his T-shirt off his body a second later. I slip a hand down his chest and then his hard stomach until my fingers hit the buckle of his belt.

"Is this another Christmas wish, Quin?"

"Not a wish, a demand." His voice is gravel.

"Oh," I breathe.

Warm, open-mouthed kisses trail up my thighs. "Fuck, these have been torturing me for hours. Every mile was too long. Every hour, excruciating . . ."

When he reaches my center, his tongue swirling around my clit, my legs fall apart for him. My hands gravitate into his hair. "I missed you, too, sweet man."

"How much did you miss me, baby?"

He nips my clit, and the moan that slips out is breathy and heartbreaking.

"Way more than I should have."

He pulls back, rocking onto his heels as his gaze studies my face. "Oh yeah? Why's that?"

I tamp down the need to roll my eyes at him. "I-I . . . just —" I suck in a parcel of air but it's too thin.

He pushes to his feet, hands clasping my face. "So you know, you have my whole heart. This man isn't going anywhere. I'm not going to bail on you at the first sign of trouble."

My chin wobbles. Why is my chest so heavy?

He adjusts his footing, closing in until his forehead is pressed to mine. "I'm not going to go out and not come back, Celeste. I'm right here. If there is one thing I can give you, it—"

I press a finger over his lips.

"I don't want anything from you, Quin."

"But what do you need, Celeste?"

It takes me a moment to realize. Then the air vanishes from my lungs, the bridge of my nose burning. He's literally on his knees asking me what I want, telling me he'll give me what I need.

It's the most intimate moment I've ever shared with anyone. He's absolutely selfless. And I . . .

Inhale a shuddering breath.

"CC, please," he rasps, hands gripping my hips.

"I—"

His head hits my stomach. I should say something. I need to say something. To tell him what I want. That it's him and Maisey and this little family that we've had a glimpse of over the last month. The tiny town that brought us together is more comforting than the prospect of returning to the city and its myriad of opportunities that I'm sure I would only burn through. It's a soulless existence.

Here, however . . .

I cup his jawline in my hands and tilt his face up. "Closer, Quinnie."

He pushes to his feet. "You need closer, baby? I'll give you so damn close, you won't be able to tell where you end and I start."

I tilt my head up now, looking into his darkened blues. "Good."

"Careful what you wish for," he groans, nipping at the soft spot beneath my ear.

I roll my head to the side with a low moan. "Quin?"

"Yeah?"

"There's tinsel in the top drawer."

He chuckles. "'Bout time I got to make use of that old canopy bed."

Nerves fling electricity through my veins at the thought of being helpless to his whims. And when he kneels again and pushes my thighs apart, running his tongue through my center, I can't fucking wait to be tethered to his gigantic bed.

Left after just one torturous sweep of his tongue, I'm gathered in his arms again before being splayed out on the bed. As he crawls over me, holding his weight above me with his hands, the clock ticks over.

12:01 a.m.

"Fuck . . ." he groans. "Merry Christmas, Celeste."

The top drawer rattles a beat later. Lengths of shining, crinkly tinsel wrap around his fist. I close my eyes for just a moment, and when I open them, Quin has a Santa hat on. But the merry expression on his face has slipped to something much more feral.

I suck in a breath and tug at the tinsel in his hand. "Knock me off the nice list, sweet man."

And he does.

EPILOGUE
QUINTON

Twelve months later . . . Christmas Morning.

Sleigh bells jingle as Maise chatters away to Caleb up on the driver's bench seat. This year, she's taken sleigh rides up a notch, insisting on being co-pilot. Co-driver?

Hell, I'm not complaining. I have a beautiful woman by my side, her head resting on my shoulder. Her smiles have been mine for twelve months, along with her soft touches and loving ways and words that have made the last year incredible. And I have a plan to make sure Maise and I get to keep her.

Hank has been doing so great in his new setting. The first two months were an adjustment, but he settled in, and his condition has been a little better. CC visits twice a week after her classes at the elementary school. After painting the backdrops for last year's Christmas play, she was commissioned to run mixed media classes for the school.

And that studio of her mom's? Well, I may have gone a little nuts with the renovation on that one . . .

"You're quiet, Quinnie," Celeste says softly, each syllable brushing past the shell of my ear as she looks up.

"Just thinking, baby."

"Yeah, what about?" She glances to Maise, who is still talking to Caleb like he's the one getting the rundown on Nickel's new harness and how to guide a sleigh over the fields Caleb grew up on.

"Nothing much, just errands."

"What errands do you have to run on Christmas Day, MacKelvie?" She raises one elegant eyebrow. Still calls me by my last name when she's being a sassy woman.

I chuckle. "You'll see."

"Hmmm. What are you up to?" Her eyes narrow and she sits up. I slide my arm around her shoulders, dotting a kiss to her temple.

Wouldn't you like to know, baby.

The sleigh ride is over ten minutes later, and Maise refuses to leave Nickel.

"Can I stay here today, Daddy? Please?"

She's hopping on the spot, her mittened hands pressed together like she's praying. Some things never change.

"It's up to Caleb, kiddo," I say.

Caleb's gaze swings between the three of us. "Sure. I could use the help." He winks as Maise gives me the 'told you' look with a tilt of her head.

"Alright, but I'll be back to collect you for lunch."

"Yay!" She climbs back up into the sleigh, settling in like she owns it.

"You two enjoy your morning," Caleb says with a shit-eating grin.

CC rolls her eyes and hooks her arm through mine.

"Bye, Daddy! Bye, CC!" Maise waves from the sleigh as we make it back to my truck. I wave back, opening CC's door, and she climbs on in. I'm around the front of the truck and in the driver's side when she says, "What will we do with hours of free time?"

"You are going to paint. And I'm running those errands."

"You're serious? You have errands on Christmas Day?"

I tamp down the smile that wants out all over my face. "Sure do."

"Well, we have guests, so the painting will have to wait a hot minute."

Pulling into the driveway, I kill the engine and hop out, crunching through the snow to CC's door. She slips out, and I catch her by the hips, claiming her mouth with mine.

It's cold out, and she shivers as I part the seam of her lips with my tongue. Our warm breath clouds between us. CC pulls away, dotting a kiss to my jawline before she tracks through the snow to her childhood home, now the Grafton B&B.

After her brother and sister went to great lengths to have Hank deemed no longer mentally capable of making legal decisions, they tried to take the house out from under Celeste. Figures . . . Only, it was already gifted to Celeste in both Trisha and Hank's wills. Apparently, after finding out that little titbit, they were too busy to contest it.

Not gonna lie, was a little happy about that plot twist for my girl.

With the inn always overrun during the holidays and the small-town charm always attracting tourists and folks wanting a quiet place to relax and recharge, we turned Hank's house into a five-bedroom bed and breakfast.

The sign that hangs over the porch swings in the gentle breeze as the love of my damn life steps up the front door and waltzes in. Warmth in my core grows in my center as a smile stretches my face. It's amazing what a difference twelve months can make. Two strangers moving to a quaint little town, neighbors who became friends . . . eventually.

And now, Celeste is—

A cold squall steals my train of thought, sending my hands into my back pockets and my feet up the steps to our house. Maise was beside herself the day CC moved in. I've never seen her so damn excited. I push through the door and into the house. The warmth of the fireplace envelops me as I shrug my coat from my shoulders and hang it on the hook by the door.

I have one task to get done before Christmas lunch and then presents.

Every year, Maise is too impatient to wait until lunch, but this year, she's been suspiciously quiet. In fact, I spotted a few random gifts under the tree that neither CC nor I bought.

My girl has a big heart, that's for sure.

I take the steps two at a time and swing around the banister, heading for my room. Inside, I hunt through the sock drawer for the last item on this year's Christmas list.

I have one task to get done before Christmas lunch and that present.

Mum, at least he appears to want until lunch, but this year he's been suspiciously quiet in bed. I spotted a few random gifts under the tree only a few months.

Mum, his absence, but I'm not sure.

I take the steps two at a time and jog along the landing, heading for my room, ready to launch into our first draw for Christmas on this year's Christmas Eve.

EPILOGUE CONTINUED...

CELESTE

Making up the bed and refreshing the towels in one of the guest rooms, I throw another log on the fire in the room's hearth. The fire crackles, warming the space. The couple will be back later today, and I want their stay to be amazing. I place a tray of Christmas-themed goodies on their bed and swap out the mistletoe for a fresh sprig above the bedroom's threshold before closing the door.

It's the little details that make the difference.

Just as true in taking care of people as it is in art.

With each room tended to, I pad downstairs and tidy the sunroom, refreshing the snacks on the buffet before pulling my coat on and heading into the backyard through the double glass doors.

The yard is covered in a thick layer of snow. Snowmen

grace the spans, built by our latest guests. And the old oak stands proud, sheltering the art studio. A far cry from the tiny shack my mother had, the new large wooden cabin-like structure was built by hand. Quinton's heart and soul went into it.

And I've never loved a man more.

He owns my heart. He has for a long time now.

I slide the large barn door open and step inside. The two small fireplaces, one either end, are lit.

Industrial lights hang over each workspace, giving off enough light that I can work at night. But I prefer to spend my evenings with my two favorite people.

I sit down on my mother's old stool, freshly uphol-stered. That was a project Maise and I undertook. Only having an hour, I make the most of it, putting the finishing touches on an oil landscape. When the last stroke is placed, I sign the corner with a small brush in black paint.

Fitting, since it's my last name and all . . .

My phone vibrates in my pocket.

Time's up.

I clean up and wander back to the B&B. Most of the guests are back for lunch. I'm setting the table as a knock rattles the door. The food is here.

I open the door for the caterers, their hands full with Christmas lunch for ten people. "Oh, it all smells wonder-ful! Come in."

With the table laid out and looking incredible, I ring the dinner bell.

Couples migrate downstairs, chatting away and laughing among each other as they take their seats. I wish them well and walk out the front door, heading for my own Christmas lunch.

With my two favorite people.

A Little More Epilogue

QUINTON
(LAST BIT . . . PROMISE!)

CC stops midstride as she pushes through the front door. "Daddy!"

Hank stands with Sandy's help. "Hello, pumpkin."

She flies into his arms. And I'm choked up, hugging Maise to my side.

"I think she's happy," Maise says, pushing up on her tiptoes.

I lean down and mess up her hair with my hand. "Yeah, she is."

And the day is only just getting started. "Alright, let's do presents and then eat before Maise gets hangry."

"I do *not* get hangry!" Maise pouts.

I gather my family and usher them into the living room.

"We're not having lunch first?" CC asks.

I nod at the sofa. "Mixing it up this year. Sit."

She takes a seat next to her father on the sofa.

Maise grabs a gift from the tree, handing it to Hank. "Merry Christmas, Mr. Black."

He unwraps the box to find a new watch. Maise and I picked that one out.

"Oh, this is wonderful . . ." A confused smile cracks on his face. Maise just beams at him before grabbing another small box from under the tree and holding it behind her back.

"Try it on," CC says. Sandy helps Hank shift his sleeve.

I shove my hands in my pocket, nerves raising higher with every minute that passes. I pace by the tree as Sandy raises an eyebrow, her head turned away from the others as she narrows her eyes.

Fuck, she's on to me.

"Here, CC. Open this one." Maise shoves the small box into CC's hands.

"Oh, sweetheart, you didn't have to get me anything." She hauls her into her arms, but Maise wriggles her way out.

A beat later, I'm being shoved closer and closer to CC, small hands in my back as Maise grunts with frustration.

"What on earth, kiddo?"

"You have to be here. But *lower*."

"What's gotten into you?" I ask.

She tugs at my sweater as CC unties the ribbon.

When she rips the paper from the box, Maise is insistent, pulling on my arm. "Down, Daddy," she whisper-shouts.

"What the—"

The paper falls to CC's lap, and I recognize what's in her hands.

A small box.

A small *jewelry* box . . .

What have you done, Maise?

"CC, open it!" Maisey chirps, her eyes narrowing as she looks up at me and tugs on my arm hard.

Celeste opens the box.

Her mouth gapes as she looks from the plastic cereal box ring to Maisey and then up to me.

She beat me to it. My own daughter beat me to the goddamn punch.

"Maise, this is—"

Maise slaps a hand over Celeste's mouth, not letting her speak. "Daddy, come on. I did the hard part for you."

I chuckle and drop to my knee.

CC's eyes widen. "Quinnie?" She's muffled against Maisey's hand.

I pull Maise to my side and whisper in her ear, "Small green box under the tree, kiddo."

Her eyes light up and she races to the tree, returning with the small green gift box. She hands it to me and steps back. The anticipation on her face is ridiculous.

I turn back to find CC clasping the small box Maisey gave her.

"Celeste, baby. Now that I've been beaten to the punch by a six-year-old . . ."

She chugs a laugh, but it peters to a sob.

I place the gift in my hand and hold it up to her. "Open it."

She swallows, taking the box from my hand. Carefully, she slides the ribbon from the box, then the paper falls away.

The black ring box sits in her hand unopened for a moment as she glances to Maise, giving her the sweetest smile. "Can I open it?"

She's not asking me.

She's asking Maise if this is okay.

"Open it," Maisey whispers.

Celeste cracks the box open. Her face twists with emotion as her eyes find mine. "Quin."

I take her hand in mine. "Marry me, CC. Let me be your constant for as long as you'll have me."

She huffs a sob and tilts her head. "Only if I can be yours, too."

"God, baby. Fucking always." I take her face in my hands and kiss her mouth.

"Daddy! So gross." Maise giggles but jumps around the sofa, cheering.

Sandy and Hank join in, even though I'm pretty sure Hank doesn't realize what's happening. Not even the point. He's here. Maise is here. And the love of my damn life just said yes.

When I release CC from a punishing kiss that promises more to come later, I find Maise staring up at me. She's smiling when she says, "Manners, Daddy. You said a bad word."

CC and I chuckle as Sandy explains it to Hank.

I bend down and hold both her hands. "Good thing I have my beautiful girls to keep me on the straight and narrow, kiddo."

"Always, Daddy."

CC leans down, and we're in a group hug. "How about you see what Santa brought?"

Maise tears off toward the tree with a squeal.

"Naughty or nice, sweet man?" CC whispers.

I plant a kiss to her neck. "Whichever means I get more time with you."

EXTENDED EPILOGUE

QUINTON

***Eighteen months later . . . A Balmy Summer's
Afternoon.***

The backyard is in full bloom, a landscape of color framed by raised garden beds overgrowing with flowers, vegetables, and the like. The beer in my hand is covered in condensation. I take a sip, the cool liquid sliding down my throat as I sit on the back porch.

Maise and Celeste run through the soft summer grass, arms held high, homemade giant bubble hoops in their hands. Laughter spills through the air as they create enormous bubbles over their heads. When one sinks, bursting over CC, she squeals.

Her small baby bump is only just visible under her pretty yellow summer dress. Maise spins, sending her bubble floating above her head. The smile that blooms over my face is followed by a low rumble of a laugh that emanates happiness.

The paper in my hand that I'd almost forgotten about while watching my girls has me content. The envelope simply has my name scrawled over the front, which means she was here. And hopefully, it's the only time she ever graces this town with her presence.

> *You win.*
> *Your daughter will never see her mother ever again.*
> *I hope you're happy, asshole.*

I can live with that.

Need more Quinton & Celeste?
Grab their wrapped up in tinsel spicy scene here!

In the mood for some cowboys? Head to Rosewood Ranch to meet the Rawlins men.

Grumpy light house, age gap with forced proximity more your vibe? Tap here!

FIRE ISLAND SERIES

Or is enemies to lovers your thing . . .

Hate to love
Big city x small town
Found family
Therapy
SASSY LOVE
Love in the city series
ALEXANDRA BANKS
thecowboysprincess@gmail.com
Charity
Slow burn
Familiar characters
You're welcome princess
Follow the arrows cowboy

ACKNOWLEDGMENTS

I have to admit, me and Christmas have been somewhat estranged over the past years. Life got busy and harder than I'd like, leaving Christmas to become just another expense that sucked the life out of our household.

But . . . as any good story does, this one reignited my love for the holiday. Seeing it for more than just a stressful time of year. It helped me focus on the people I love, and celebrate making it through another year together.

I hope it can help you do the same.

As always, thanks to my editors, Lindsey and Zainab. Your input and guidance is always wanted and appreciated.

To every *ARC reader* who volunteered to read this book, thank you!!

Til next time beautiful . . .

Alex xx

ABOUT THE AUTHOR

Alexandra Banks is a romantic at heart, and an optimist down to her very bones. Her love for everything romance sees her writing HEAs all day long.

But don't be fooled, there will be angst along the way, possibly heartbreak. But her fierce heroines can handle just about anything!

For more heartwarming reads, follow her on socials and join the mailing list so you never miss another heart throb!

9 781764 342315